THE HORSE CONNECTION PART 2

horses, friendship and revenge

THE HORSE CONNECTION PART 2:

horses, friendship and revenge

© 2025 Charlotte Godfrey
All rights reserved
ISBN *979-8-9913993-5-7* paperback
ISBN *979-8-9913993-6-4* ebook
ENOLA PUBLISHING LLC

A previous version of this book was published in 2014 under the title
DRESSAGE LESSONS © 2014 Charlotte Godfrey
It has been revised, re-written, and re-named to become the second novel of
THE HORSE CONNECTION series

THE HORSE CONNECTION part 2 is a work of fiction. The characters in this book are fictional, and not based on any person, living or dead, with the exception of Craig Heckert, owner of Rivervale Farm.

EXTENDED TROT

Irene's story
was originally published as a novelette in 2024
© Charlotte Godfrey
ENOLA PUBLISHING LLC
all rights reserved

TABLE OF CONTENTS

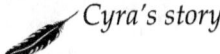 *Cyra's story*

EXTENDED TROT

Irene's story

3

DEDICATION

For Dawn, Mikey and Deb. You opened your hearts to me. I was surprised and grateful. Thank you.

1 - THE SHOW

It was the second week in June and the day we would take our horses to the show grounds for the first sanctioned show of the season. For most of the boarders, including me, three shows a year would be enough, financially or time-wise. However, those who were chasing awards, medals or trying to qualify for Regionals might have to compete in five or more shows this year.

Some of the boarders, lesson people and working students would be going only to schooling shows with their young or lower level horses. Bonnie didn't coach at the schooling shows, and didn't attend most of them. That was Layne's job. But both Bonnie and Layne went to the sanctioned shows and coached their students who attended them.

This was my first sanctioned show and I couldn't decide if I was excited or scared. It was a two day show, which meant that the horses would be on the show grounds for three days. On the first day, the horses would be trailered into the show grounds and horse stalls and tack stalls would be set up. Then the horses would be taken out to the show grounds and exercised or just led around so they could look at their new surroundings and relax.

It was noontime and we were preparing for the trip to the showgrounds at Waterloo. Bonnie and Layne were checking their lists. Twelve horses would be going to the show and all three of the farm's trailers were hooked up to trucks and filled with feed and hay, water buckets and feeders, tack, fly sheets and emergency first aid supplies.

The show grounds were almost two hours away, near Jackson, so nothing could be left behind. Twenty four sets of polo wraps littered the floor at Bonnie's feet, all of them white and wrapped in tight rolls, four to a set. Twelve hay bags lay behind Layne, filled with sweet-smelling second cutting hay. Saddles, saddle pads, girths, bridles, whips, lunge lines, side reins and exercise boots had already been loaded onto the trailers.

"Did you put all the paperwork on the horses in my truck?" Bonnie asked Layne. "The Coggins, the USDF and USEF registrations, memberships, etc.?"

"Yep!" Layne declared.

"Okay, then. That's it. I think we can load up."

I was standing beside an un-made up, un-pierced Cyra. I had arrived at 10 am, after packing all my show clothes, casual clothes, snack food and other miscellaneous and probably unneeded items. When I got to the barn, I ran around offering help to everybody and anybody until Cyra pulled me aside.

"Do you have your show clothes, your casual clothes and your personal stuff ready?"

"Yes," I answered.

"So, you're all set, and your car is gassed and ready to go? Your horse's legs are wrapped, his helmet is on his halter, and he has his sheet on?"

"Yes,"

"Then stand back and wait," Cyra told me. "You'll just get in the way and slow those two down if you don't. They've done this a zillion times and they've got it under control. Just wait for orders."

"Okay," I said, feeling like a child.

Cyra wasn't kidding. A few minutes later Layne started barking orders. "All right, people, please pay attention! After we get the polo wraps loaded we will hang the hay bags and then load the horses. Your name will be called. If you have more than one horse going to the show, you will be told which horse to load first. You might not be loading your second horse on the same trailer, so pay attention!"

I felt like saluting. Cyra did and clicked her heels together. I laughed and glanced at Layne to see if she would be angry or treat Cyra's gesture with humor. When Layne called out sharply, "Cyra!" I jumped, sure that a reprimand would follow.

Cyra bounced a little on the balls of her feet. "Be right back!" she said to me and hurried over to where Layne was standing. Instead of reprimanding Cyra, Layne began grabbing bundles of polo wraps and Cyra did the same. Soon, all twelve sets were stored on the three trailers parked outside the barn. Next, six hay bags were hooked into the first horse trailer.

"Ben!" Layne called out. "Get Caesar and load your horse."

Ben turned and went to get Caesar.

"Martin! Bring out Julius!"

Ben appeared with Caesar, who was wearing royal blue shipping boots, a gold trimmed royal blue show sheet with his name embroidered in gold on it and a protective head bumper on his halter. Martin followed with Julius, dressed in the same outfit, of course, but with his own name embroidered in gold on his sheet.

After Caesar and Julius were loaded without a fuss, Layne called out: "Connie! Bring out Chance first and then Zip!"

Real and Chimmy were loaded last in the trailer, the doors were closed and the ramp was lifted and latched. Layne threw the keys to Cyra and said, "Drive carefully."

I looked at Cyra. She smiled and said, "Do you want to follow me with your car?"

"Uh, yes. I didn't know you were driving..."

"There's a lot you don't know, my dear," Cyra said in a Groucho Marx voice, wiggling her eyebrows and knocking ashes off an imaginary cigar.

I followed Cyra and the trailer to the expressway entrance. When both vehicles were settled into the flow of traffic on I-94, I called Cyra on her cell phone. "Why didn't you tell me you were driving? I assumed you would ride with me."

Cyra laughed. "I drive to every show. That way, Bonnie doesn't charge me transport fees or for the tack stall. I braid and groom, so I make some money that way, too. When we go to Florida I will probably drive one of the rigs."

"Well, that's great," I said, but I was disappointed. I had anticipated driving to the show together. "I'll let you concentrate on driving. See you there," I said.

"See you there," Cyra repeated.

I settled back in my car and reminded myself that I was very lucky. I had a wonderful car and a privileged life. But it seemed like I was always alone.

Al was away again. This time in New Jersey. He told me a little about the case. He and his team were defending a man accused of murdering two men who had, reportedly, raped his daughter. Al had left the morning newspaper open on the breakfast nook table for me when he came home to pack his suitcase. I was still at the barn when he left for New Jersey, so I didn't even get to tell him goodbye.

I shivered. The whole thing made me feel ill. How could Al work each day with people in such horrible situations?. I appreciated his effort to share a little of his work with me. Knowing something about what he was doing helped me tolerate his absences and excuse his tiredness. Even though I didn't get to spend as much time with him as I would like, and even though I still had occasional doubts about his faithfulness, knowing just a little about his day-to-day work helped me be more patient. I was willing to wait until Al proved to me "who he is," as my mother would say.

My mother taught me to be patient. Although she wasn't a religious woman, in the sense of following the beliefs of a particular religion, she taught me that the Bible is a wonderful book of wisdom. One of my mother's favorite biblical quotes was Matthew 7:20 "by their fruits ye shall know them." This, she told me, meant that you can tell who a person is by what they do, not what they say. When someone did something unethical or dishonest Mom would say, "Well, now we know who THEY are!" So I was willing to wait to see who Al was, and also who Cyra was.

It was 3 pm by the time we arrived at the show grounds. By 3:30, the other two trailers had arrived. Layne was driving the second trailer, hauling four horses and Bonnie drove with Danielle, hauling Bravo and Woodsman, in her two-horse trailer with living quarters.

After unloading the horses and gear, the six and four-horse trailers were parked in an area designated for that purpose, but Bonnie parked her trailer in the camping area of the showgrounds, next to the stables.

"Bonnie stays right on the showgrounds with the horses," Cyra told me. "She checks on them during the night and even has an security camera hooked up so she can watch them when she's in her trailer."

"Oh! I thought she would be getting a motel room like the rest of us," I said.

"Nope," Cyra replied. "I stay on the showgrounds too. I sleep in the tack stall and help her keep an eye on the horses. I'm up half the night braiding anyway, so why go to the trouble of driving off the show grounds and spending money on a room I'll use for, maybe, four hours a night?"

"Oh." I was disappointed. I had imagined free time with Cyra, laughing about the events of the day and planning things for the next day, but that wouldn't happen.

After the horses were unloaded and set up with water buckets and hay, everyone helped unload feed, hay and tack under Bonnie's watchful eye.

Show management had given Centerline Farm two rows of stalls, seven in each row, facing each other. Two stalls were designated by Bonnie as tack stalls. Irene and I watched as Bonnie, Layne and Cyra hung burgundy stall curtains with the Centerline Farm logo embroidered in gold on them. Burgundy stall door panels, also with the Centerline logo, were hung on each of the twelve horse stalls. A piece of burgundy carpet was put on the ground in front of the two tack stalls, and gold director chairs were set on it. A table draped in the same burgundy material was placed in the center and two gold ropes were hung in front of the tack stall curtains.

"What are the ropes for?" I asked.

"To hang our ribbons, of course!" Irene told me impatiently.

I cringed. Of course. It was common practice to hang ribbons in front of stall curtains at sanctioned shows, but it wasn't as common at the schooling shows, where I had shown. Why did I ask that dumb question? And why did I have to ask it in front of Irene?

When Bonnie was satisfied with the stalls and their decorations, she asked everyone to join her in the tack area. From under the table, she brought out a bucket of ice with a champagne bottle buried in it and Layne opened a box of plastic champagne glasses.

"I'd like to share a toast with all of you to celebrate the beginning of our show season," Bonnie said to everyone.

Cyra and Layne passed out champagne glasses as Bonnie popped the cork on the bottle. She poured champagne for everyone and said, raising her glass, "Here's to us, after months of diligent work with our horses! Let's have a wonderful show season!"

"Hear, hear!" "Cheers!" and "To us!" echoed through the group as we touched our glasses together. I noticed that Irene did not reach out to touch anyone's glass. They reached out to her and touched her glass instead.

After taking the horses out to stretch their legs and get a look at the show grounds, everyone except Cyra, had dinner at the motel restaurant. Bonnie ordered a carry-out for Cyra and I volunteered to take it to her.

Cyra was braiding horses when I got to the barn.

"Thanks," she said through a mouthful of rubber bands. Yarn and white pieces of cut tape hung from her apron. "I'll finish Woodsman real quick and eat while it's still warm."

"Do you want me to hay or anything?"

"It's done."

"Oh. Well, do you need anything?"

"I need a lot of things," Cyra laughed, "but nothing here."

I smiled. "Well, I guess I'll head down to the motel room. I'm rooming with Danielle, you know."

"Yep. I suggested it."

I didn't reply. Being with Danielle was almost like being alone. I scratched Real's withers and left Cyra to her dinner and her work.

Layne and Irene had private rooms next to each other, and I saw "Do Not Disturb" signs on their doors. Ben and Martin shared a room next to theirs. Connie and her husband had a room across the hall and the room I was sharing with Danielle was next to theirs.

Danielle was a thin sixteen-year-old who had only once said "hi" to me and that was when we were first introduced to each other. She constantly wore her iPod, using only one ear bud, in case someone had something to say to her, but she rarely spoke. I put my toiletries in the bathroom, took a shower and went to bed with a book, hardly noticing the quiet young girl who seemed to not notice me either.

Danielle was finishing up in the bathroom when I woke up at 6 am the next morning. I washed my face, combed my hair, and met the others for breakfast at 6:30. We didn't talk much because everyone was thinking about their classes for that day. Even the twins were quiet. Danielle and I fit right in with the quiet, self-occupied group.

Bonnie, Layne and Irene weren't at breakfast with us. When we got to the show grounds barn shortly after our breakfast, I saw that Layne had tacked up Irene's horse. I watched her help Irene get into the saddle. Parcel was quiet, looking a little bored. He seemed to reflect the withdrawn and aloof expression of his rider.

Irene, Parcel and Bonnie walked down to the warm-up ring. Layne followed them, carrying Irene's dress coat and a towel.

I looked at the ridetime schedule posted outside the tack stall. Irene's first class started at 8:11 am.

Ben and Martin started grooming their horses, brushing their chestnut bodies to a gloss, combing their flaxen tails, and tacking them up. Connie and Danielle were doing the same with their horses.

I didn't have to ride a test until 11 am, so I checked on Real, making sure he had fresh water and hay, and then went to find Cyra. At Chimmy's stall, I found her sound asleep, sitting in the back corner of the stall. Chimmy was braided, and her blue-grey coat was sparkling clean. She was eating hay at Cyra's feet. I folded my arms over the half door of the stall and watched for a while.

All twelve horses were braided, and I knew Cyra must have been up all night since each horse required 30 to 45 minutes to braid. Wearing no make-up or piercings, and with her black hair hanging over her eyes, she looked like a child, sitting in the corner of her horse's stall, sleeping. I smiled and left her to dream.

By the time I got to the warm-up ring, Irene and Parcel were outside the ring. Layne was wiping the dust off Irene's boots and the foam off Parcel's mouth. Bonnie put her hand on Irene's knee and said something to her She made circular hand gestures with her left hand and Irene nodded.

Bonnie steped away from Irene and Parcel and Layne handed up Irene's shadbelly coat. She watched as Irene put it on and buttoned it over her stock tie. Then she dusted Irene's boots one last time and gave her a thumbs-up.

Irene turned her horse and walked to the show ring. Bonnie, Layne and I followed. We waited for the rider in the competition ring to finish her test, clapped politely and wished Irene good luck. Irene entered the outer ring and circled it at a trot until the judge rang her into the competition arena.

Irene was riding an Intermediaire I test. All went well, except for a slight loss of balance going into the canter pirouette to the right and a late start in the tempi changes. It was an unexciting but good test. Irene came out of the ring with a smug look on her face and Bonnie and Layne breathed a sigh of relief.

"Good job!" Bonnie told her.

Layne patted Parcel and wiped the foam off his mouth. "You did a great job!" she told Irene.

Then Irene looked my way.

It took me a moment, but I understood. "Good ride," I said.

Irene didn't smile, but I saw the corners of her mouth move.

There was no one else to give her praise, so Irene urged Parcel away from the ring and back toward the barn. Bonnie stayed behind to coach Danielle and Layne and I followed Irene and Parcel back to the barn.

Halfway to the barn, Irene leaned down to Bonnie and asked, "Did my husband call?"

Layne shook her head.

"Did you check all the calls on my cell phone?"

Layne nodded.

Irene frowned. "Well, I will leave my phone with you. When he calls, tell him dinner will be at The Meadows."

Layne nodded again and said, "Will do!"

At the barn, Irene dismounted and left Parcel with Layne. "I'll be at one of the tack trailers," she told her.

Layne saw my puzzled look and said, "Irene is nervous. She shops at the tack trailers when she's nervous."

I held Parcel for Layne while she untacked him and put his sheet on. Then she grabbed a flake of hay, checked his water bucket, and put him in his stall.

"Okay. he's good." Layne said. "I'm heading over to coach Connie. Wanna come?"

"Sure."

We walked back to the warm-up ring so Layne could coach Connie, but I drifted over to watch Bonnie coach Danielle. Danielle and I were sort-of roommates, so I felt a kind of loyalty to her, instead of Connie.

A few minutes later, I saw Irene walk over to Layne, a bulging shopping bag over her shoulder. She wasn't smiling as she leaned against the rail and watched. I saw her turn her head to Layne and say something I couldn't hear.

Layne just shook her head.

Irene was in a sour mood until, a few minutes later, the results of her class were announced. Irene received a score of 64% and took the blue ribbon. I watched Irene straighten her back, smile at Layne and high-five her.

Danielle and Connie rode their tests at almost the same time. Danielle was in Ring 1, riding Prix St. Georges and Connie was in Ring 3, riding Fourth Level test 3. I stood with Bonnie and watched Danielle ride her test quietly and with precision.

"She will get a good score," Bonnie said.

We clapped as Danielle exited the ring and got a tiny smile from her.

The twins rode in Ring 2, both riding Grand Prix.

They were scheduled to ride one after the other, and it was like watching a re-run when Ben followed Martin into the arena. Everyone laughed when Ben purposely blew his one-tempis in the same spot where Martin's horse had fumbled his one-tempis.

Ben came out of the arena and rode up to Martin, who was still mounted and waiting. Both horses and riders bowed to each other, the riders removing their top hats with a wide sweeping gesture. Bonnie and I clapped and laughed, and other spectators and riders joined in the fun until the ring steward frowned and asked us to "take the party elsewhere."

I was scheduled to ride in less than an hour, so I made my way back to the barn. Cyra was heading down to the ring and waved when she saw me.

"Hey, I was just coming to get you! Real is saddled. He's ready to go."

"You didn't have to do that."

"No, but I wanted to."

"Well, thank you!" I gave Cyra a one arm hug, and I was happy when she didn't shake it off. She just smiled.

At the barn, I checked Real's saddle and bridle to make sure Cyra had fitted everything correctly. "Good job," I said. "He looks great. Thank you."

We walked together to the warm-up ring. I led Real, and Cyra walked beside me, carrying my coat and a towel.

Layne was waiting by the fence, talking to Irene. She was my coach for the show, and I felt encouraged by her presence, but I was a little self-conscious about warming up in front of Irene.

I took Real to the ring's mounting block and got on, then walked him once around the ring. Soon, I forgot about Irene and just worked with my horse. We trotted, put in a few serpentines and leg yields, then shoulder-ins. We cantered, and I was pleased with Real's prompt obedience and his good attitude. He seemed happy to be at the show and I thanked my lucky stars once again for finding me such a happy, talented horse.

At the end of my warm-up Layne simply said, "Good."

"Thanks," I said. Irene was looking away from Layne and me, with her hand on her hip, posing again. Then I realized that she had turned her back on Cyra, not me.

Cyra was standing by the fence, holding my coat and the towel. I walked Real out of the warm-up ring and over to her. She handed me my coat and said in a quiet voice, "You look great."

"Thanks."

I dropped Real's reins and put my coat on. Real stood quietly as I buttoned my coat and adjusted my stock tie. "Is the tie okay?"

Cyra nodded, and I picked up the reins again. Then she wiped Real's mouth and dusted my boots. We walked together to the show ring and I noticed that Real matched Cyra's stride. Layne and Irene followed us at a distance.

When it was time to enter the ring, Cyra wiped my boots once more and said, "Go show 'em how it's done!"

I grinned at her and entered the outer ring at a trot, waiting for the judge to ring us into the competition ring for our test.

We trotted in front of the judge's booth and the scribe nodded to us and smiled, but the judge was busy finishing her comments on the previous rider's test. We turned the corner past the judge's booth and headed down the long side toward the entrance to the ring. The judge rang the bell before we reached the corner. Real and I turned the corner and entered the ring in a smooth sitting trot.

Then it was like tunnel-vision for me. It was just me and my horse. I wasn't aware of the judge, the scribe, or the spectators. Real was supple, relaxed and obedient. We rode our test happily together. Only when we halted and saluted the judge, did I notice everything around us again. Real dropped his neck and we walked from the ring on a loose rein and I couldn't stop smiling.

Cyra was grinning at us. "That's the way it's done!" she said when we reached her, and I laughed.

I dismounted, and we headed back to the barn with Real. We didn't talk. It wasn't necessary. We were smiling and happy.

I had just finished topping off the horse's water buckets and Cyra had given the horses more hay when the results of our test was announced over the loudspeakers. Real and I had won first place and earned a 72% for our 2nd level test. I gasped and froze in place with the water hose straight up in my hand. Cyra jumped up and down, hi-fived the hose, and we broke out in laughter.

Cyra's ride was scheduled for 2 pm. After we grabbed a quick lunch from one of the food vendors, I helped Cyra tack up Chimmy. We wrapped her legs for the warm-up, saddled her and, while Cyra slipped on her riding boots, I bridled the mare.

I ran my fingertips over the rows of laced braids in Chimmy's long mane and touched the browband Cyra had made with turquoise beads and a small feather woven into the center.

I grabbed Cyra's stock tie and folded her shadbelly coat coat over my arm. Then we walked Chimmy to the warm-up ring where Bonnie was waiting to coach Cyra. Chimmy warmed up beautifully, as always, and Bonnie didn't say anything except "Ya, ya, good."

Chimmy seemed to have an extra spark at the show, like most of the horses from Centerline and I wondered if the horses, like their riders, felt excited to show off what they had learned.

Soon it was time to enter the ring. I handed Cyra her stock tie and coat. Then I wiped the foam from Chimmy's mouth and the dust from Cyra's boots. As Cyra entered the outer edge of the competition ring, I said, "Go dance!" and Cyra grinned at me.

And dance they did. Cyra and Chimmy performed their Prix St. Georges test with energy, precision, and beauty. As they left the arena, the announcer told the audience, "This little mare's breed is called Nokota. You don't see many of them in dressage competitions. They are descendants of Spanish horses turned feral in North Dakota. Indians in that area captured some of them, learned to ride them, and used them to attack the foreign invaders who had released them."

When the announcer said that Irene turned to Cyra with a sneer on her face and Cyra put her hand behind her head with two fingers sticking up like feathers. Then Cyra pointed her feather fingers at Irene. Irene's face blanched, and the sneer fell away.

Cyra and I left the competition area. Most of the day's classes were over and we untacked Chimmy and worked together, bathing our horses.

Chimmy was getting a final rinse when the class results were announced. Cyra had won her class and had also received a 72%. I high-five her with the hose and we, once again, broke out in laughter. For the rest of the afternoon, we grinned and called ourselves the "72 percenters."

2 - DINNER WITH JOEY

Irene's husband arrived at dinnertime. Everyone, even Cyra, gathered at The Meadows Restaurant to have dinner together. Tomorrow afternoon, the show would be over, and everyone would be packing up to leave. Dinner would consist of left-overs from the concession stand on the show grounds or snacks bought at stops during the drive home. But tonight, we would feast and celebrate the events of the day.

The restaurant was packed, so we gathered at the bar for drinks, and stood in a circle and talked as we waited for our table. A few minutes after our drinks were served, Irene's husband walked into the bar area. He was spotted first by the twins. "Joey!" they cried in unison.

"Hey-hey!" Joey answered, patting them both on the back and squeezing them together in a hug. "What's zup?" Joey wasn't overweight, but he was big, although shorter than Al, who I suddenly missed. Like Al usually did, he wore a dark suit. But Joey's tie, not like Al's typical tie, was wide, bright and multi-colored. It seemed to add a cheery note to the already festive atmosphere.

"Irene's up!" Layne answered. "She has her first score for her Gold Medal! Only three more to go!"

"Hey, hey, hey, Layne!" Joey gave Layne a hug and looked for his wife in the crowd. Finding her, he pushed through and grabbed her.

"Irene! Babe! You did good!" He hugged and kissed her loudly, not noticing that she looked uncomfortable.

Then he spotted Bonnie. "Bonnie! How are you, my love?" Bonnie got a hug too.

Joey looked around. "Where's our table? Why aren't we seated? Didn't you call in a reservation?" His questions weren't directed at anyone in particular, so no one answered, and Joey didn't wait for an answer. "Wait here. I'll be back," he said to no one in particular.

"That's my Joey," Irene said with a little smile as she watched him disappear into the crowd.

"Yeah, he'll get us a table and fast!" Layne said, laughing.

I watched as Joey approached the hostess at the desk. He asked her a question, and she shook her head. Then he asked her another question. She looked at him. He shifted his weight and put a hand in his pocket. The hostess consulted her table chart and looked up. She said something to Joey, and he smiled, put his hand on her shoulder and gestured toward the dining room with his other hand. The hostess picked up a stack of menus and Joey took them from her, putting something in her hand as he took them.

Then Joey walked back to his wife. "Okay! We can eat! Follow the young lady!" Joey waved us toward the smiling hostess.

We were given a large round table at the back of the restaurant. Without a doubt it was the best table in the restaurant and, also without a doubt, it was because Joey made it happen.

"Thanks, Joey," Bonnie said and raised her drink to him.

"Here, here!" seconded the twins and everyone raised their glass to Joey.

"So!" Joey said. "My Irene did good today, and we're gonna celebrate her one-fourth gold medal! Order what you want to eat and drink. It's on Irene!" Joey looked at Irene and she smiled and nodded her head.

"Cheers!" shouted Ben and Martin and raised their glass to Irene. The rest of the table, including Cyra, raised their glass and toasted Irene.

"So! Now I want to hear from the rest of you - what you did today!" Joey said and pointed to Connie, who was seated next to him.

Connie looked around the table at each of us. "Well," she said, "I don't know if any of you noticed, but Chance lived up to his name. He was pretty tense going into the warm-up ring and bucked twice. On the second buck, he actually unseated me, and tossed me onto his neck! Fortunately, he stopped when he felt me clinging to his neck and let me to slide back into the saddle. After that, he settled down and warmed up normally. We went into our class and took second with a score in the high sixties."

Layne, who had coached Connie in the warm-up,

laughed and said, "You handled him very well and your score was 69%. Don't be so modest!"

"Well done!" Bonnie said.

Connie blushed and laughed. "Next, please" She nudged Danielle, who smiled and looked down at the table. "Woody was a good boy," she said quietly.

Each person at the table took a turn telling Joey about their rides and the funny or interesting things that happened throughout the day.

When it was Cyra's turn to tell Joey about her day, she shrugged and said simply, "Chimmy did pretty good for an Indian pony!" Irene choked on her sip of wine and Cyra nodded at Ben and Martin, indicating that it was their turn to speak.

I could see that Joey was an influential man. He obviously had money and knew how to use it. I could understand how he could sweep a pretty model off her feet and overwhelm her with his energy, his money and his joy of living. Al had that effect on me.

I also could see that Irene loved Joey by the way she watched him with quiet pride and a half-smile on her face. Her eyes hardly left the man, even when the twins were telling, comically, their version of the events of the day.

I glanced at Cyra. I was astonished to see that Cyra was wearing the same expression as Irene. Only Cyra was watching Irene, not Joey. Throughout the dinner, I kept watching Irene and Cyra. Irene watched Joey with an expression of contentment, and Cyra watched Irene with the same expression. What was going on with Cyra?

Back at the showgrounds after dinner, Cyra started checking braids. Real's braids were intact and did not require fixing, but a couple of the other horses needed touch-ups for the next day. I watched as Cyra's expert hands made the repairs. When we moved on to Parcel, Cyra began taking out his braids.

"What's wrong? They look fine!"

"They may look fine now, but by morning, they will be a mess!" Cyra said. "Trust me, this horse is high maintenance, just like Irene!" Cyra laughed. "It's best to go ahead and take them out now, let him scratch a little, and do him again early tomorrow morning!"

After the remaining horses' braids were checked and repairs made, we fed them more hay and topped off their water buckets. Then Cyra picked the stalls while I raked the aisle and filled hay bags for the morning.

When we were finished, Cyra turned to me and said, "You'd better get back to the motel and get your beauty sleep. Tomorrow morning comes early."

"I hate to leave you here," I complained.

"Are you kidding me? I can't wait for you to leave so I can relax!" Cyra laughed. "Go on! Go!"

I smiled at her. "Why don't you come to the motel and sleep in a real bed tonight?"

"No. I'm okay. I like being with the horses! Really."

I shook my head. "I believe you." I turned to go, then stopped. "Would you mind if I camp out with you at the next show? I mean, I'd really like to, if it's not imposing on you."

Cyra looked at me and smiled. "I guess that would be okay. It's not the most comfortable arrangement, but the port-a-johns are clean and they let us use the shower in the office."

"Okay, that sounds like fun! I'd like to hang around the horses too. I wouldn't go back to the motel tonight if I weren't rooming with Danielle. I feel responsible because she's so young and no one is here for her. What's her story, anyway? She never talks to anyone."

"It took me a while to get to know her, too. She's the only child of a college professor and his wife, who is a computer programer. She has a form of autism called Asperger's Syndrome. It's not severe. She just has problems communicating with people and she's a bit clumsy at times. Her parents gave her riding lessons to help her physically, and she became obsessed with dressage. That's another symptom of Asperger's. Obsessions. She's obsessed with music too. She's doing a musical kur tomorrow."

"I know. I can't wait to see it."

"Yeah, well, don't ask her about it unless you have two hours to listen to her talk about it in detail! And without looking at you the whole time!" Cyra laughed.

"That wouldn't be all bad," I smiled, thinking of how Al wouldn't or couldn't talk to me. "See you early tomorrow morning, then."

Sunday was a repeat of Saturday, weather-wise, and the show results for Centerline Farm were just as pleasant. The twins played at their Grand Prix Special tests and earned a decent score and a scolding from Bonnie, who told them, "If you two would get serious, you could be a real sensation!"

"Naw," Ben replied, "That would be boring!"

"We decided that we're gonna open up a dinner and performance theatre with horses! THAT will be fun!" Martin told her.

"I think you will do very well at that," Bonnie laughed.

I rode my qualifying test for Second Level and left the ring with a huge smile. Real had been perfect in every movement. I came out of the ring and saw an equally large smile on Cyra's face.

"Bore - ring..." the twins chimed as I dismounted and everyone burst into laughter.

Irene rode Intermediare II later that morning and Cyra rode Intermediare II after the lunch break. Unlike yesterday, Cyra was in the same class, competing with Irene. When the results were tabulated, Cyra took the blue ribbon for the class, with a score of 68%, leaving Irene in second with a 63% and in a nasty mood.

Joey had stayed overnight to watch the show on Sunday and laughed at Irene's bad mood. "Maybe you should sleep with the horses too, Irene," he said.

"Maybe you'd do better then?"

Irene countered with, "I already sleep with an ass, remember?"

Joey guffawed and slapped his thigh. "Good one!" he said and got a smile from Irene.

The Musical Freestyle rides were the last class of the day. Five riders had registered to compete in this costumed "fun" class to close the show.

Cyra and I stood on a little hill by the ring to watch. I looked around, and it seemed that everyone at the show had gathered to watch the class.

The first rider was dressed as Inspector Clouseau. Her horse was draped in pink, and they danced to the theme music of The Pink Panther.

"That was great!" I said, clapping.

"I should have planned a ride for Chimmy," Cyra said. "I can see her dancing to drums..."

The twins followed and performed a "mirror dance," each using half the arena. Their music was a custom mix from the album "Here's to Future Days" by the Thompson Twins. We laughed when they concluded the ride by backing up to each other and saluting the judge and the audience.

The next competitor dressed as Wonder Woman. Her horse wore the shield of Superman on his chest and Superman theme music accompanied her vaulting skills.

I thought of how Cyra mounted and dismounted

Chimmy on our trail rides. "That was amazing!" I said. "Cyra, you could do that! I mean, the way you jump on and off Chimmy, you could do that!"

Cyra just smiled.

Danielle was the last to ride, and she had chosen Klaus Balkenhol's Spanish music from the 1994 World Equestrian Games. As she and Woodsman pranced in the arena, the spectators started to clap in rhythm to the music, at first quietly, then louder when they saw it was not upsetting her horse. By the time Danielle finished her routine with a halt and a salute at X, all the spectators were clapping loudly in time with the music. Her parents, who had arrived that morning to watch the show, were beaming. Danielle left the arena with her head bowed and a smile on her face.

Each competitor in the Musical Freestyle class received a blue ribbon and a basket of gifts from local businesses.

The show was over. Trailers were loaded with tack and left over supplies. Quietly, and with a touch of sadness, everyone gathered their belongings and took down ribbons and stall banners. When everything was packed and loaded in the trailers, stalls were cleaned and the horses were loaded. A stream of trucks, trailers, and cars left the show grounds in a quiet and orderly parade.

I followed behind the trailer driven by Cyra and thought about the show and about Al, who was still in

New Jersey. It was a long, lonely drive home.

When we arrived at Centerline Farm, only the horses were unloaded. Bonnie left the equipment and supplies to be unloaded by the working students on Monday.

I helped Layne and Cyra feed the horses and, after brushing Real and adjusting his sheet, I reluctantly left the farm to drive home to my empty house in Grosse Pointe.

3 - CYRA TELLS HER STORY

I took Real from his stall, put him on crossties and started my grooming routine. Real stood quietly and leaned into the rubber curry when I found an itchy spot. After the currying, I brushed his coat with a medium bristle brush followed by a soft brush. I was brushing his tail as I had been taught, from bottom to top, when Cyra walked up.

"Hi, Cyra. What's on your schedule today?"

"Riding, then work. Nothing special."

Cyra's tank top was turquoise and neon pink. Her black hair was streaked with turquoise and pink and she had black riding breeches and boots on. Her eyes were blackened, as usual, and her lips were neon pink.

"What do you add to that outfit when you work?" I asked with a smile.

"Not much. Mostly, I take things away." Cyra smiled. "I do three different performances each night. The less I wear, the more I make. I just put on a short skirt, a scarf or a shawl, maybe fuzzy leg warmers and I wear a g- string,not a c-string."

"A c-string? I know what a g-string is. What's a c-string?"

"It's like a cup that covers the front and goes in back like a thong, but nothing over the hips. I don't like c-strings because there's no place to stick a tip - you know - money. They can't touch a c-string, but they can tuck money under the g-strings on my hips."

I just frowned at her explanation.

"I'll have to show you. Or you can look online."

"They really sell that stuff online?"

"Sure. They sell g-strings, c-strings, pasties, bras, tear-away stripper costumes, make-up, false eyelashes, even stripper sunglasses!" Cyra laughed.

I just stared at Cyra, then shook my head. "I've got to get out more," I said with a smile.

"You said you're coming to see me perform some night. Did you mean that?"

"Sure, I mean, if you don't mind?"

"Not at all. Get ready for an education, my friend! When do you want to go?"

"Um. What's good for you?"

"Saturday night has the best performers. Sunday night is quiet, and more private. Suit yourself."

"Well, Al is usually out of town, so it doesn't really matter."

"Okay. I will take you as my personal guest on a Sunday night. I'll take you backstage so no one will bother you and you can watch the girls get dressed before they undress! Or," she looked at me sideways, "You can go with Layne. She's at the club a lot. But, it's a secret. She doesn't want anyone here to know."

I was trying to figure out what that meant when Irene walked up.

Cyra turned, faced Irene and said loudly, "Maybe Irene would like to see me work sometime? You could take her with you."

Irene gave Cyra a cold look, then turned to face me. She tilted her head back slightly and said, "Watch yourself. You should be careful who you hang with."

Before I could respond, Cyra said, "Ah ha! I see you've got a pair of sneaky shoes just like Layne's! Did you buy them together, or did you buy them for her?"

Irene blushed and said in a low voice, "It's none of your business, you little whore."

Cyra seemed to puff up and said, "Watch yourself, Irene! You may have everyone else fooled, but I know what YOU are!" Cyra was bristling with anger.

I looked from Cyra to Irene, whose face was flaming red. Irene was at least four inches taller than Cyra and, in her riding boots, she seemed six inches taller. She moved in close to Cyra and leaned over a little until she was nose to nose with her. Looking directly in Cyra's eyes, said in a low, quiet voice, "You keep away from me and keep your trashy mouth shut - or I'll shut it for you."

Cyra returned Irene's stare and repeated in a low growl, "I know what YOU are." Seconds passed. I watched the two women frozen and staring at each other, their bodies rigid and hatred in their eyes. I was relieved when Irene broke the stare, turned abruptly and went into Parcel's stall.

I took a deep breath and looked at Cyra. It seemed

that Cyra had deflated. She had been standing on her toes in an effort to match Irene's height. She brought her heels down and rounded her shoulders. Her fists had been balled up in anger, and she slowly opened her hands.

Cyra looked at me. "She's my sister," she said flatly.

I blinked. "What? What do you mean?"

"Yeah. She's my sister. But she doesn't know who I am."

My heart was pounding. I heard it in my ears. I didn't understand what Cyra meant, and I found it hard to breathe. Finally, I asked, "Do you want to go for a ride and tell me about it?"

A few seconds passed while Cyra stared at the floor. Then she looked up at me. "Yes," she said.

As our horses walked along the trail, I listened to the sounds their feet made on the dry dirt. Dandelion puff balls waved to us in the gentle breeze. When we entered the shaded areas of the trail, I saw that the wild foxglove plants had flowered. I took a deep breath and I could almost taste the cooler air around us.

"I love walking along, seeing everything, smelling everything and hearing the sound of a horse's feet on the trail," I said.

"Me too," Cyra said. "Few things make me happier. I love the sound of horses munching hay, too." After a minute, she said, "And I love the sound they make when they get their hay. First, they blow a little through their noses. But, if it's really good hay, they sometimes make a bubbly noise."

"Yes," I smiled, relieved that Cyra was talking, "It sounds like when you blew bubbles in your drink as a kid, and your Mom told you not to!" I laughed, but when I saw Cyra frown, I stopped laughing.

We rode on in silence. After a while, Cyra said, "I trust you. You've shown me that you are a true friend."

"Cyra! What's going on? What happened back there?"

Cyra turned Chimmy around to face me. "Let's ride to the meadow," she said. "When we get there, if I still feel the same as I do now, I'm gonna tell you everything."

I stopped breathing, and my eyes were suddenly stuck open. I couldn't breathe or blink.

Cyra turned Chimmy in a half pirouette and urged her into a canter. I shook myself, then cantered Real along the trail and up to Cyra and Chimmy, who had stopped to wait for us.

When I caught up to them, Cyra turned Chimmy and led us down to the stream. At the edge of the stream, she stopped and jumped off Chimmy. Then she walked into the stream and fished out two rocks, gave one to me, pushed one into her breeches pocket, and walked Chimmy through the stream. Real and I followed, picking our way through the stream and to the meadow where Cyra and Chimmy waited for us. I got off Real and slowly approached Cyra, not knowing what to expect.

Cyra frowned at me and said, "I'm sorry I seemed to doubt you. I haven't trusted anyone since I was a kid."

"I've never given you any reason to doubt me," I said. "But you don't have to tell me anything. I don't need to know your story."

Cyra looked at the stream, then at me. "I need to tell someone, and I trust you. I've been carrying this around for so long, I need to unload. Are you willing to carry some of it with me? It's gonna hurt you."

"How could it hurt me?"

"It will change you. Nothing comes without a price, believe me. Decide now. Please."

I looked at Cyra. "You can tell me."

"Okay."

We walked slowly through the meadow and let the horses snatch mouthfuls of grass.

Cyra took a deep breath. "Irene is my sister, but she doesn't recognize me. We got separated a long time ago, and she has a different father than mine. She's tall, I'm short. She is elegant, and dresses like the rich bitch she has become, and I dress like the stripper I am. The last time she saw me, I was ten years old. I've changed a lot, so she never guessed."

I was confused and opened my mouth to speak, but Cyra held up her hand. "When I was ten, she came to get me. She was eighteen and beautiful. She told our mother that she was taking me to a better life. I think our mother believed her. I believed her. Irene certainly looked prosperous. She drove up with a man in a Cadillac and gave our mother a thousand dollars. That was a fortune to our mother." Cyra dropped her head.

"So I went with her. She took me to a house where she left me to work for eight years. I had to stay there until I was eighteen." Cyra looked at me, not blinking. "It was a whorehouse. She sold me to a whorehouse. A whorehouse with children."

"What?" I couldn't breathe. I couldn't think.

"Yeah. The whores were children. She sold me to a whorehouse. I became a whore."

Finally, my brain fired back, "What? That's illegal! I know that prostitution is legal in most counties in Nevada, but never with children!"

"But that's what it was. We were all supposedly adopted by the owner of the house. This woman, the owner, was a woman who had gone through the same kind of thing back in the seventies, and she knew how to work the system. She paid off a lot of people. But she was making a lot of money, so she could afford it. Creeps will pay a lot of money to be with a child." Cyra turned away from me and looked across the meadow.

"How many children were there?" I didn't really want to know, but I knew Cyra needed to tell me.

"Usually five. Sometimes more. I don't know where they went when they left. She had boys and girls."

"And they were all there to be..." I couldn't finish.

"To be prostitutes. Mostly for men, but there were a

few women, too. We were forbidden fruit for the rich."

I was speechless. I looked away from Cyra. Then I looked back. "Why didn't you run away?"

"I did. The old woman just sent someone to get me. She knew where I would go. Where else would I go? I ran to my mother. I went quietly back with whoever was sent for me because I couldn't tell her what Irene had done. It would have hurt her too much. And I felt ashamed. I felt dirty." Cyra looked down at the grass. "I still do."

"Cyra, don't. You didn't choose that life."

Cyra looked across the meadow. "My mother died while I was there. I didn't know. I found out about it the last time I escaped and ran home." Cyra balled up her fists. "I vowed to find Irene and make her pay."

"I don't understand how they could keep you there against your will," I said.

"It was easy. Somehow, that woman became my legal guardian. I don't know how she did it, but all the kids were adopted. She probably paid off people. She changed our names. My name was Enola, and she changed it to Cyra. Most of the kids didn't have any place to go. Or they were staying there to keep her from grabbing one of their brothers or sisters. That's what she told them: You run, and we will find you and take your brother or sister, too."

"That's sick," I shook my head. "But you didn't have a brother or sister left at home. At least she couldn't use that against you."

"Yeah, but she told me she would get my mother fired from her job. I didn't know if she could do that, but I was afraid she could."

"What about school?" I said. "You went to school, right? Couldn't you get help there?"

"No. We took classes and did our schoolwork on the internet. They said we were home-schooled." Cyra sighed. "We were schooled, for sure."

Cyra stroked Chimmy's neck. Then she turned to me. "We used the internet for school. When I learned how to search on the internet, I thought I might be able to find my sister. But I had to sneak it in. I couldn't let the old bitch know what I was doing, but the kids covered for each other and we knew how to erase our internet history."

Cyra sighed, then continued, "So I found her. Eventually. It took a long time. I just kept Googling her name, every day, day after day. I never stopped. One day our last name showed up on the internet in a few pages. Our name was Pamahas. We are from the Painte tribe, but I don't know much about that, really. I left when I was ten, and my mother never said much about our history. She never said much, anyway. We just worked and tried to survive."

Cyra looked at me, and her lips smiled, but her face was sad. "I found our name after almost a year of searching. I found it in the results from a dressage show. She had changed her Indian name. It was Ituha. She changed it to Irene and, when she married, she hyphenated her last name with his, like some high-class bitch! Irene Pamahas-Cutone." Cyra shook her head and her lips were pressed together in a thin line.

"I couldn't believe I had finally found her. I wouldn't have been sure, even then, but there was a picture of her on the website, and I remembered how she looked when she was eighteen, when she came to get me, and I recognized her. I knew I had found her."

Cyra took a deep breath, then continued, "I didn't even know what dressage was, but I looked it up on the internet and found out. I decided to learn dressage someday, and find my sister."

"So you could get revenge?" I asked.

"Sure," Cyra looked at me.

"Is that your 'mission'?"

"It was," Cyra admitted, looking away. "I was hurt and angry. I wanted to kill her. But now, I just want to know why she did it. Why she sold me and abandoned our mother. Yeah, I wanted to kill her." Cyra bit her lower lip and stared at the clump of meadow grass at her feet.

"I would probably feel the same," I said.

"Well, Irene can be a real bitch, but I don't hate her anymore. I think she could be a nice person if she would let herself. Have you seen how she is with Joey?"

I nodded.

"She really loves him. She likes Bonnie and Susan and Layne. She's pleasant to other people."

I raised my eyebrows.

Cyra shook her head. "She's only snotty with you because you're nice to me. I treat her like crap because she looks down on me. And because I'm still angry and hurt," Cyra admitted, frowning. "But I can't hate her. Every time I see her, I know she is my sister and our mother loved both of us. She never said a bad word about Irene, ever." Cyra wasn't crying, but a couple of tears had rolled down her cheeks.

"What happened after you found her?"

"Learning about dressage became my obsession. I read everything I could find on it. I watched dressage on YouTube when I could sneak it in. I followed her show results on the internet. I imagined myself doing dressage. One day, on the internet, I found a lesson barn in Reno, advertising dressage lessons. It was only 20 miles away. I talked the old bitch into letting me go there for lessons once a week in exchange for 'special favors.' That, and I think the fact that it looked good to anyone who might check up on her, convinced her. She had one of her goons drive me there, once a week. The lessons were basic, but it was a start and I knew that was the way I'd catch up with my sister."

Cyra stroked her mare's neck. "That's where I met Chimmy. One of the boarders at the barn owned her. She was a 3-year-old filly, and I watched them do ground work and then train her to saddle. I wanted her." Cyra smiled.

"A couple of years later, I found an online article about amateur riders breaking into FEI levels, and it mentioned Irene Pamahas-Cutone." Cyra spit Irene's name out slowly. "Itt said that she trained with Bonnie Heins. So I searched for Bonnie Heins, dressage trainer and found her biography on the internet. It gave the name and location of her barn, and I made a plan. I thought that, when the time came, I knew where to go. I was almost old enough to make my move."

"What move?"

"To get free."

"How did you do it? You left before, but you said they always brought you back." I was holding my breath, afraid to hear what Cyra would say next.

"I was almost eighteen. She had to let me walk out the door when I was eighteen. Legally, I was free then. So I told the old bitch I was leaving and that I wanted my savings."

"What?"

Cyra snorted and nodded. "The old bitch said the same thing, What savings? And I said, I've worked for you for eight years. I want fifty percent of all I've made."

I couldn't breathe.

"She laughed at me. So then I took out a notebook and showed her the dates and the amount of money I collected for her for each 'transaction' in the last year. Then I told her to multiply that by eight."

Cyra shook her head. "She slapped the notebook out of my hand and said that it meant nothing. She said that for all she knew, I had been whoring behind her back all the time while she was trying to provide a decent home for me!"

I choked and gulped a bit of air.

Cyra smiled. "So I told her that I knew about the hidden cameras in the rooms."

"Hidden cameras?"

Cyra nodded. "I found the camera in my room after seeing spy cams on the internet. She had them put there so she could watch us with the customers. Maybe to blackmail the customers too. I don't know. But I learned how to hack into the cameras and copy the feed. After that, I picked a few fights with her and her customers. She slapped me and yelled. The 'customers' would get angry with me and say incriminating things. I reminded her of those times and told her I had recorded them. I told her exactly how I had hacked into the cameras and that I had saved the last year of the recordings on a remote website and that I sent a link to my sister, who had married a very wealthy and influential man."

"Wow," was all I could say.

"I told her that, unless I got my money, the footage would be sent to the police, and I would make sure she spent the rest of her life in jail."

"Weren't you afraid? Didn't you say she had guys to keep you the other kids under control?"

"Yes, she did, and she reminded me of that, but I told her my sister's married name and told her to look her husband up on the internet. When she saw who my sister had married, her eyes told me she understood that my threats were real, and she knew she had to let me go or I would ruin her."

Cyra shrugged. "It was a bluff, but it seemed to work. I hadn't contacted my sister. I hadn't sent anyone copies of the videos. But I had stored the videos on two places on the internet and I gave her the web address of one of the places and the password to it and invited her to look. I told her that she could destroy or delete those files because I had copied all of them to another website and my sister had those files. That finished it. I got most of the money I demanded from her, and I was told to leave immediately."

"Wow."

"I was still afraid that she was gonna have her goons do something to me after I left the house. Maybe even kill me. My knees were shaking as I walked out the door, but I had to risk it. I had to get free with a large amount of money to find my sister. Nothing else mattered to me."

"So, you just walked out? Where did you go?" I was gripping Real's reins so hard my hand hurt.

"Well, I didn't just walk out the door. I had arranged for one of the guys from the lesson barn in Reno to pick me up. I told him the day and time I would confront her, but not about her. I didn't want him to try to be a hero. He would only get himself hurt and spoil my chance of escaping. He was there right on time. Not one minute late and waiting outside. He was a pretty tough-looking guy, and I guess it was enough for her to let me walk away. She probably thought she would find me later."

"Where did you go? Did you try to contact Irene?"

"Hell, no! She didn't want me! She SOLD me to the old bitch! The last thing she wanted was for her little sister to show up and mess up her new life! She still doesn't know who I am!"

"Oh." I rocked back on my heels. "So, what did you do?"

"I went back to the stable in Reno and bought Chimmy. I offered the owner so much money, she couldn't refuse, and the barn owner got a real nice commission for calling her and making the deal right there on the spot."

"Did you get the stable owner to drop you and Chimmy off here?"

"No. I looked in her phone booth and hired a guy 50 miles away. I didn't want any connections the old bitch could follow."

"And Irene didn't recognize you."

"The old bitch had changed my name to Cyra, and Irene hadn't seen me in eight years. I had grown up a lot. And I got these." Cyra pointed to her breasts. "No one in our family had boobs. Not even me. When I hadn't grown any by the time I turned sixteen, the old bitch decided I needed these."

Cyra stopped talking. We listened to the horses, tearing at the meadow grass, chewing. A little yellow butterfly landed on Cyra's arm. It opened and closed

47

its wings, then flew away.

"What will you do now?" I asked. "Will you get revenge for what Irene did to you? Is that the mission you said you needed to get going on?"

"That was my plan in the beginning. To get revenge. I spent eight years in that place because of Irene, and I wanted to get even with her and the old bitch too."

Cyra sighed and threw her arm over Chimmy's back. "Now I don't care. Now all I want to do go to Florida for at least one season. That's my mission now. I'm okay with Irene. I just wish she wasn't such a bitch."

"Well, I think she's a bitch because she's never been happy. She's never figured out how to be happy. Maybe she thought marrying money would do it, but it didn't."

"You're probably right. Maybe that's my revenge."

"Are you gonna be okay?"

Cyra scratched Chimmy on the neck and sighed. "Yeah. I feel better now. Thanks for listening. I think I just needed to tell someone."

"Well, you were right. Now I feel awful."

Cyra looked at me.

"For you. And for Irene."

Cyra nodded. "I get it. Well, let's go visit the statue, tell her our troubles, and then go back to the barn. I've gotta go to work."

We rode to the statue in silence, placed our stones in the ring and stood for a minute, then remounted and rode back to the barn in silence.

48

4 - FRUSTRATIONS

I didn't know what Cyra was feeling, but I was sad. She was right. I paid a price to hear her story, but I was glad she shared it with me. I hoped I had relieved her burden a little by listening.

We put our horses in their paddocks, and Cyra left for work. I told her I would put our tack in the tackroom so she could leave and run a couple of errands before going to work at the club.

I grabbed my saddle, pad, and our bridles. I almost collided with Layne when I entered the tackroom. She was standing just inside the entrance, pounding her fists on the wall and muttering to herself.

"Layne! Are you okay?"

"Oh! I'm so angry!" Layne spun around and frowned at me. "Kathie just quit!"

Kathie was a working student and she had been at the farm for a less than a month. In that time, I watched Layne patiently show her how to clean stalls, tack up, untack, cool out, bathe and turn out horses.

Layne's face was red. "She quit. Said she wasn't going to clean a sheath! She wasn't asked to clean one! I was just showing her how to do it. I thought she should know. It's part of a male horse's care. You can pay the vet do it, but you should know when it needs to be done and how to do it." Layne's face got redder as she continued.

"She said she wanted to train. She wasn't interested in daily care and maintenance. We give all the working students a thorough education in the care of horses, but she wanted to ride all day and become a trainer within a year!"

I shifted on my feet. My saddle, pad and the bridles were getting uncomfortable, but Layne didn't seem to notice. I wiggled the saddle up a little and rested it on my hip. That made holding it a little easier. It was clear that Layne had more to say, and I was her captive audience.

"When I told her it takes years of mucking stalls and working around horses, as well as riding them to become a good trainer, she thought I was kidding! When I showed her how to clean a gelding's sheath, she got upset, and when I told her she needed to learn how to do it, she quit! She said I was insulting her."

Layne was so red in the face I couldn't stop looking at her. The longer Layne ranted, the angrier she got. I had no idea how to calm her.

I laughed nervously.

That seemed to anger Layne even more. She balled up her fists and spit out, "What's so funny? I had to do all that and more! I spent years slaving in barns so I could get where I am now! I'm still kissing butt to get where I want to go!" Layne's eyes had narrowed to slits and her face was bright red. Her body was hunched forward at me, and for a moment I was afraid and took an involuntary step backward.

Layne instantly understood that she had frightened me and said, "I'm sorry. I shouldn't take my anger out on you."

"I didn't mean to upset you," I said, stepping back toward Layne. "I know teenagers can be frustrating."

"You don't know how many working students I go through here. I don't even want to take them anymore! None of them have the faintest idea of what it takes to become a trainer. They think you buy the clothes, buy the horse, ride and win at a few shows, then people pay you big bucks to be their trainer!"

Layne shook her head. "It's quicker to become a doctor or a lawyer." She looked at me. "You have to do the daily grunge work and put your butt in the saddle for hours and days and month and years! It's just plain hard work and they don't get it!" Layne was starting to sweat.

"How many years have you been working at it?" I asked gently, hoping to calm her.

Layne sighed and slumped against the wall. "I started taking riding lessons when I was nine years old, riding western on an old rank horse in exchange for feeding horses and cleaning stalls. They didn't know I was nine years old. I told them I was twelve and they believed me, maybe because I was tall. Or maybe they didn't care. When I was really twelve, I found a job at a barn and took more lessons from that owner, but I got into trouble and kept getting fired. The owner's son was always making trouble. He was three years older than me, and it got worse and worse."

Layne's anger was focused on her past now, and I watched as she folded her arms around herself, telling me about her younger years. Then she took a deep breath and straightened her body. "When I was fourteen, I got a working student position with Craig Heckert, and things got a lot better. No one harassed me. I mucked stalls, I groomed, I ran errands, I helped harvest and stack hay, I carried heavy bags of grain, I did anything! I got to ride, I got lessons, and I got a small salary."

I nodded at Layne, encouraging her to continue.

"I got a salary and, when I graduated from high school, I got an apartment above the barn. I stayed there for 6 years, longer than most people spend in college getting a degree! I paid my dues in sweat and hard work. I got a great education and a guarantee of nothing but hard work, no health care, no social security and uncertain wages for the rest of my life, but I wouldn't trade it for anything." Layne managed a small smile.

I saw that Layne's face was returning to its normal color. Talking about herself and how much she loved the life she had chosen was starting to calm her. Hoping to continue to calm her, I asked, "So where do you see yourself ten years from now?"

Layne smiled and unfolded her arms. She pushed

away from the wall, put her hands on her hips and looked up at the tackroom ceiling. "I see myself in my own training barn, with lots of horses in training and lots of people taking lessons. I'll have students working for me, cleaning stalls, taking care of the daily tasks of feeding and turnout and I'll be the one people want to become like, who they want to ride like. But not in ten years. It has to be sooner than that. I've paid my dues."

I chuckled, "Well, I'm already one who wants to ride as well as you ride!"

Layne frowned again. "I've paid my dues," she said. "I want my own barn more than anything!"

"So, is that how Bonnie got there? Did she put years in as a working student?" I asked.

"Hell, no!" Layne growled and turned to look at me. "Her mother had this barn and Bonnie grew up in it! She went to Europe and took lessons, and her mother bought her horses! She was never a working student. She earned her medals on horses other people trained, not like I have to do it!"

"Oh, so I guess people can buy their way up?"

Layne nodded her head, "Yeah. Some people have it made. Others, like me, have to fight their way up!"

I dropped my head. I didn't know what to say then. I did not know how to comfort Layne. Money had its advantages. In every profession, people without money fought hard to climb a ladder that the rich didn't even know existed. It was easy for me to see that Layne's frustration with the working student was really her own frustration with life not being fair.

"Well, no one's life is perfect. Not even Bonnie's, though it might seem that way. You just do the best you can and find ways to enjoy what you have."

Layne sighed and dropped her shoulders. "I know you're right, but sometimes, it's almost too much."

I agree, I thought, frowning. I found it hard to forget my own troubles. Al had come back from New Jersey, but he hadn't been home early all week. He told me he was working late, but when I called his office, I got no answer. When I called his cell phone, it went straight to voicemail. Sometimes he called me back within a few minutes. Sometimes it was hours later. When he finally came home late at night, he smelled of cigarettes and, sometimes, heavy, musky smells. I wanted to follow him, but knew it was impossible. I was thinking once again about hiring a private detective.

5 - THE CLUB

On the following day Layne was riding Fortunate when I entered the ring with Real to practice my Third Level test. Although we shared the arena, we rode in silence, concentrating on our horses. But when we untacked, Layne walked up to me and stroked Real's neck.

"Do you want to ride Rodney, the young horse you rode on the trail with me? I have two more horses to ride, and it's good for you to ride other horses."

"Sure, I always want to ride. Thanks!" I said and Layne smiled.

"You're good company," she said.

I wondered where Irene was, and, for the second time that day, I wondered where Cyra was. "Have you seen Cyra today?"

"No, why?"

"She was a little down yesterday. I just wondered."

"Well, let's ride, then do barn chores and go watch Cyra at work!"

"At the strip club?"

Layne laughed, "Where else?"

"Okay, I've always wanted to see Cyra perform," I said. What I didn't say was that I would feel confident going to the club with tall, aggressive and self-assured

Layne, who, Cyra said, had been there before.

I rode Rodney and helped Layne with evening chores. Since Al hadn't gotten home before midnight all week, I just texted him and said I would be home later than usual, and, if he needed me, I would have my cell phone turned on.

It took us a half hour to drive to the club where Cyra worked. I realized too late that I should have driven my own car and followed Layne since the club was closer to my house than the barn. Now I would have to ride back to the barn with Layne and get my car, then drive home. But it was too late, and it probably wasn't important, so I didn't say anything.

Layne parked her car on the side of the cinder block building, after waving off the baggy-pants kid posing as a valet.

"There are no valets here," Layne told me, laughing. "Just kids trying to make a buck. Or steal a car!"

"Really?"

"It happened one night when I was here."

I rubbed the goosebumps that suddenly appeared on my arms and thought maybe it was good that I didn't drive, after all.

I looked at the side of the building and could feel vibrations coming from it through my seat in the car. The music being played inside was heavy on bass. Neon tubes on the front of the building flashed the name "X-odus." My goosebumps didn't go away.

The building was garish, painted the turquoise color Cyra often wore in her clothing. Rectangular in shape, both short sides pointed to parking lots. On the back side of the building there was a large garbage dumpster and, in a fenced, padlocked area, stacks of empty crates and a storage building.

As we walked across the parking lot, Layne locked her car with her key fob, causing it to beep, and I jumped a little. The parking lot surface appeared greasy and irregular, made of asphalt that would heat up during hot summers and become brittle and cold in winter. Every few steps, my shoes stuck on something and make a sucking sound as it released me.

To cover my nervousness and muffle the sucking sound, I said, "You've been here before?" Layne had found the club easily and had driven in as if she were a regular.

"Don't blab, but yeah. They have Amateur Night here, and I've made quite a bit of money doing it!"

I gasped before I could stop herself. Then I laughed. "Amateur Night? You? Really?"

"Don't be shocked. My husband is usually here. We need the cash. He watches out for me. And you can't take it all off, so he doesn't feel jealous. Actually, I think he feels kind of proud. I'm not too bad to look at, and it makes a few bills disappear!"

"Layne, I feel so ignorant! I never knew about this stuff. Did you strip in South Dakota?"

"Heck no! In the first place, I didn't even know

about strip clubs then. And in the second place my mother and Craig would have killed me!"

"Your mother and your boss would have killed you, but your husband is okay with it?" I laughed but felt a little weird. Layne seemed like an intimidating stranger again. I longed for simple and true friends, but people were constantly surprising me. They were complex, and it was scary.

"Yeah, well, there weren't any places to dance in South Dakota. None that I knew of then, anyway."

Outside the club door, Layne was greeted by the bouncer who was sitting with one leg propped on the bottom rung of his stool. His muscular arms were folded over an equally muscular chest, and his t-shirt sleeves were rolled up to expose his tattoos. His bleached hair was encased in a red hairnet, drawing attention to his pierced eyebrow.

"Layne, baby!" he cried, jumping off the stool and hugging her. "Where you been, doll?"

"Busy! Taz, this is my friend, Marsha."

Taz looked me up and down, head to toe. "Nice," he said.

"Not for the show. Just visiting. We came to see Cyra, okay?"

"Sure. She goes on in a few. Lot'sa tables tonight. Take your pick," and he opened the door for us.

"He likes you," Layne said. "He didn't ask you for a cover charge!"

"Oh" was all I could say as I stumbled behind Layne

into the dark club. But my eyes adjusted quickly and when Layne asked me where I wanted to sit, I pointed to a table on the right side of the room. It was almost hidden by darkness and a half-wall.

"Shy, eh?" Layne teased me. "Okay, go sit. I'll get us some drinks. We won't get a waitress here anytime soon because we aren't men!"

Layne headed off to the bar, and I walked quickly to the table and sat down.

On the stage, an almost naked blonde appeared to be finishing her routine. She had red pasties with fringe covering her nipples and red bikini panties on her bottom. She was gyrating to the music and sliding her hand into her panties. Several male patrons walked up to the stage and poked money in them. As the music ended, she gave a little shake to her breasts, the fringe flew in circles, and she turned around and bent over to give a backward bow to her audience.

The announcer jumped on stage after her exit and said, "That was Marilyn, folks. She's here on Tuesday, Thursday and Saturday nights. Next up: Daddy's Little Girl!" and he made a swooping gesture to his left as the music, probably on a CD, switched to an innocent-sounding child's tune.

A brunette with her hair in ringlets ran on stage, dressed in a short, blue plaid skirt and a white blouse with a round blue collar and blue bow tie. She also wore white stockings and black patent leather shoes.

She was carrying a large cylindrical lollipop,

and licked it slowly with one of the longest, pinkest tongues I had ever seen. The tongue snaked in and out of the girl's mouth, then around and around the lollipop, circling it as she swayed to the music. The music stopped. Suddenly, her tongue split apart and both halves encircled the lollipop. I gasped. I had never seen a split tongue before.

The music changed to something familiar and more mature, but I couldn't name it. Layne arrived with two bottles of beer just as the girl turned sideways to her audience and threw her head back. Then she plunged the lollipop into her throat, in and out, like a sword swallower, while running her free hand up her leg to her crotch. Her movements were synchronized to the beat of the music.

I accepted a beer from Layne and said, "Thank you," but my eyes quickly returned to the dancer. She had placed the lollipop in her teeth and proceeded to run both hands from her knees to her crotch, up and down.

The music got noticeably more mature at that point. The dancer began to gyrate her hips as she untied the bow and took it off, wrapped it around her hips and ran it through her legs. She threw it into the audience and started massaging her breasts through the white blouse. She shook her breasts, and the blouse came off. It was also tossed into the audience. Her pink bra was cut so low that her breasts were almost spilling out. The music become heavy on bass and loud.

Daddy's Little Girl ran her hand under her skirt and whirled around and bent over to reveal bare buttocks. Her hand was between her legs, holding that area. Her audience was moaning and encouraging her.

"Take it off!" I heard someone call out. Others in the audience began clapping to the music, which had developed a steady, pumping beat.

Daddy's Little Girl whirled around, wiggled her hips, and the skirt fell off. She kicked it into the crowd. She was wearing a g-string and began pushing her hips to the audience in time with the pumping beat. Men walked to the edge of the stage and began filling her string with money. She removed the lollipop from her teeth and began licking it, gyrating suggestively as the men continued to fill her string with cash.

When the music ended, she was wearing a skirt made of money. She bowed to her audience and her boobs, nipples covered by little white bows fell out of their inadequate bra cups and her audience moaned. "I'll be back to get my clothes, boys" she breathed at her audience, to which someone responded, "Yeah, come get 'em!"

The announcer came back on stage and said: "I'll let you catch your breath, folks, and get a drink or two. After a short break, our next dancer will be Queen Evil!"

"That's Cyra," Layne told me. "I wonder who's working with her tonight."

"Working with?" I was afraid to imagine what kind

of work Layne meant.

"You'll see. It's always a little different. Depends on who it is." Layne looked around the club. "Not much going on tonight. Usually, the place is packed. I guess word got out about the shooting."

"What shooting? Here?" I stopped breathing.

"Yeah. Last week, a guy got belligerent. He was handling some of the girls and being really obnoxious. Showed everyone his penis at one point. Jay, he's the owner, asked Taz to remove him and the guy pulled a gun. Jay tried to disarm him, and the guy got shot. Just blew a hole in his thigh but he's suing Jay! Imagine that! You get shot with your own gun after you started waving it around in a bar and you have the nerve to sue!" Layne shook her head. "Jay called me and let me know what happened."

"Did he tell you who the guy was?"

"No, Jay just said that he was in a whole heap of trouble."

"Jay or the guy?" I sank a little lower in her chair. What in the world was I doing here?

"I didn't ask. Drink your beer!" Layne scolded me. She leaned closer to me. "It will help you relax."

I put the bottle of beer to my lips and drank a sip. I squeezed my eyes shut. It was bitter! I looked at Layne, but Layne hasn't noticed my reaction to the beer. She was busy looking around the room, trying to see who was in the crowd. I put the bottle down on the table and sat back in my chair.

Layne grabbed her beer and finished it. "Hey, I'm going for a refill. Want another one?" she asked.

"No, I'm fine," I said. "Are you running a tab?"

Layne laughed, "Heck, no. I get my beer free. If you're okay, I'll just get one for me and be back in a minute. Cyra should be on soon."

"I'm fine."

Layne jumped up from the table and went to the bar. I watched as she walked right up to the bartender, who must have seen her coming because he already had a beer in his hand and was holding it out to her. She grabbed the beer and said a few words to him. He laughed and walked away. I watched as Layne walked over to a group of men at the end of the bar. One of them put his arm around her waist and pulled her close to him. She removed his arm and said something to him, gesturing with her beer bottle as she spoke. The man and his friends laughed, and Layne turned and walked back to our table.

Just as she sat down, the announcer came back on stage, and said, "And now, Queen Evil." He walked offstage and the music started quietly, sounding a little like bed springs squeaking. A woman's voice could be heard, breathing softly with the music.

Cyra put one leg, draped in a purple scarf, past the stage curtain. She raised her leg slowly and pointed her toes, held her leg high for a moment, then lowered it and cartwheeled onto the stage. The scarf fluttered like a flag on her leg and fell away.

Cyra's face was fully made up with blackened eyes, eyebrows, and black lips. All her piercings were in place, including one in her navel and two big rings hung from the pasties covering her nipples. She was wearing another transparent scarf as a skirt, a black g-string underneath it and nothing else.

The pulsating music grew louder as she faced the audience, her legs spread. With her hands on her hips, Cyra pumped her pelvis forward in time to the music, undulating her stomach and pushing her crotch at the audience. The music stopped, Cyra stopped undulating, put her hands on her breasts, lifted them and moaned. The music started again, accompanied by female breathing and sounds of "Uh, uh, uh."

Cyra released her breasts, raised her arms and began a series of slow back flips, her legs moving over her body, then her arms moving over her legs in slow motion. The audience watched quietly. I wondered if they were afraid to breathe, like me. I couldn't take my eyes off her.

"It's no wonder she's so good on horseback. Look at her!" I whispered to Layne.

"Yes, she's an athlete," Layne said.

The music grew louder.

Cyra held her last back bend for a few moments, exposing her g-stringed crotch to her mesmerized audience and flipped over slowly. She landed by a pole on the stage and placed her hands on the pole.

Supporting her body with her arms, she wrapped her legs around the pole and slithered to the top. When she reached the top, her hands left the pole, and she leaned back and slowly rotated around the pole, moaning in time to the throbbing music.

She straightened and grasped the pole again with both hands. Then she slid down it, bending away at the bottom in a slow back flip. The transparent scarf came off. She grabbed the scarf, one end in each hand, and brought it under her boobs, offering them to her audience as she strutted toward them. The music stopped.

Abruptly, she whirled away, cartwheeled across the stage, and almost disappeared behind the curtain. Only her leg and pointed toes could be seen.

I sat up a little, wondering if this was the end of her act.

The pulsating music was playing, quietly. Cyra backed up. Her mouth was open. She was pulling the scarf, but it was caught on something behind the curtain.

Cyra tugged on the scarf and a blonde woman, naked except for a g-string and a bra, stumbled onstage. The purple scarf was tied around her neck.

I choked on the beer taste in my mouth. My eyes were wide open, and I couldn't breathe. Was this a fight brought on stage? Did Cyra collide with this woman backstage as she exited?

Cyra pulled her across the stage. The woman seemed frightened and turned away, trying to escape.

Cyra grabbed her torso, whipped her around, and tore her bra off.

I jumped in my seat and looked quickly at Layne.

Layne's eyes were riveted to the women on the stage. I looked at the audience. They were silent, watching Cyra and the blonde woman.

Cyra grabbed the woman's arm and folded it behind her back, which pinned her almost bare chest against Cyra's. Cyra rubbed her body against the woman's body, and I realized that the music had gotten a little louder.

Cyra loosened her grip on the woman and bent her knees a little. She moved her head and licked the woman's nipples with her tongue. Her audience was spellbound.

I exhaled. The music had gotten louder.

Moans could be heard coming from the audience. Cyra licked the woman's breasts again, then lifted her head and kissed her, keeping enough space between their lips so that the audience could see her tongue sliding in and out of the woman's open mouth.

My eyes were dry, frozen open. More moans came from the audience.

The music had changed. The bass had increased to a heartbeat throb.

It appeared that the seduction had worked on her victim. Cyra dropped to her knees and slowly licked the air in front of the woman's crotch.

Bigger groans came from the audience.

Then she stood and placed one of her legs between the woman's legs, grabbed her buttocks and began to move slowly in time to the music.

Someone in the audience found their voice, and I heard, "Oh yeah, do her, baby," accompanied by more moans.

The music grew louder, and more female moans and breathing could be heard. Suddenly, the music climaxed with a crash of a cymbal. The women froze, then melted apart.

Two seconds later, the music came back with the "uh, uh, uh" beat, and the blonde woman grabbed the purple scarf from the stage floor and ran behind the curtain.

I could feel the audience, like me, began to breathe again.

Cyra strutted across the stage, moving her hips in time to the music, and pushed her g-stringed crotch at the audience. The audience moved toward her and stuffed money into her g-string as she pushed her hips toward them.

Cyra moved around the stage, collecting tips. Sometimes she moved her leg over the men's heads. When the money looked in danger of falling out, she pulled it from the strings and massaged her boobs with it, making room for more tips. More moans came from the audience.

One of the men near the stage stood up and held a bill in front of Cyra's g-string. I could clearly see his face. Al pushed the money in Cyra's g-string, then sat down again.

I gasped without realizing it and Layne said, "Yeah, she makes a lot of money with that number! Men are fascinated by a lesbian act."

I looked at Layne. "That's my husband," I said.

Layne sat back in her chair. She looked at me and saw the shock on my face.

"Do you want to leave?"

I sat speechless, staring at Al.

"Marsha?" Layne touched my shoulder.

I shook my head. "Not yet. I don't' want him to see me."

"Okay. But I don't think he will turn around. You're safe!" Layne tried to joke, but my face was frozen.

As we sat there in silence, Cyra came out to the bar area, dressed in a robe, got herself a drink and strolled over to stand next to my husband and another man.

Layne turned to me. "That's Jay, the club owner."

The man Layne identified as Jay had been talking to Al before Cyra stepped up to them. Jay put his arm around Cyra, and soon the three of them were huddled together in conversation.

"Okay. Let's go!" I told Layne and pushed my chair back and stood up. Without waiting for her, I walked to the door. Layne was right behind me, and we exited the building without being stopped.

Taz jumped up from his stool as we exited. "Hey, leaving so soon? I didn't get a chance to let Cyra know you were here!"

"Good," I said. "I would appreciate it if you didn't let her know."

Taz looked at Layne and raised his eyebrows.

Layne told him, "Don't let her know."

Taz saluted Layne, folded his arms over his chest, and sat back down.

We drove back to the barn in silence. When we got there, Layne parked and turned to look at me.

I was staring straight ahead. I opened the car door without looking back, got out of Layne's car and got into my car.

Layne drove away.

I sat in my car. I stared at the steering wheel and sighed. No detective was needed. I put my key in the ignition, started the car and drove home.

When I got home, I took a shower, dressed in my pajamas and was pretending to sleep when Al slid into the bed next to me at 3 am. He was sound asleep within minutes, but I couldn't sleep. What was Al doing at the club? With Cyra? What was going on?

Tomorrow, I would confront him and Cyra.

6 - CONFRONTING CYRA

By 5 am I was tired of trying to sleep. I got out of bed and turned on the coffee pot. When the coffee was ready, I poured a cup and took it out to the patio. It was late June, but it felt like July.

I sat down and thought of last winter, when I had no horse. Snow covered everything for months. Then I bought Real. The snow left and the rains of April woke the flowers in the garden. Crocuses bloomed first, followed by grape hyacinth, daffodils, tulips and bluebells. Lilies bloomed next. Now that June was turning into July, daisies and geraniums would take over. Things were always changing.

I sighed and turned away from the garden. Today, I would have to confront Al and Cyra. I had grown fond of Cyra. In fact, she was my best friend. We had a lot of fun together. Lots of laughs, but now I felt numb. It would be hard to talk to her. Even harder would be the talk I would have with Al.

I decided to talk to Cyra first. Then Al. Was this the end of a friendship and a marriage? What would be left? My mother. My horse.

It was Wednesday. I always visited my mother on her day off, and recently, she had changed it to

Wednesday. I checked the time on the kitchen clock. 5:15 am. She would be awake. Miss Priss, monster cat, wouldn't let her sleep in. In spite of my troubled thoughts, I smiled and picked up my phone.

"Marsha?"

I heard the surprise in my mother's voice. "I know it's early, but that's why I called. Let me take you to breakfast." I listened to her protest and interrupted, "Feed Miss Priss, brush your hair and get dressed! I'll be there in 45 minutes. Bye."

I finished my coffee, rinsed out the cup, washed my face, pulled on my riding clothes and was out the door before Al woke up.

Richmond, Michigan is a city with a long history. In 1835 it was known as Beebe's Corners. In 1859 the Grand Trunk Railway was completed and the area prospered by supplying lumber and agricultural goods during the years of the American Civil War. In 1878 Beebe's Corners merged with Ridgeway and Cooper Town to form the Village of Richmond, and in 1966, Richmond became a city. In 1989, the city expanded to include Muttonville and eventually annexed parts of Lenox, Casco and Columbus Townships. Over 5,000 residents live in the city of Richmond, but it has the structure and atmosphere of a much smaller town.

My route was directly opposite the main flow of traffic that morning. I arrived in Richmond slightly ahead of schedule and stopped to buy flowers. Then I drove down Main Street, turned right at Division and right again into a driveway by the side of a big white house. My mother's apartment was above the garage, behind the white house.

Climbing the stairs to the apartment, I noticed that the stairs and the porch had been painted. There was new tread on the stairs and a new table with two new chairs on the tiny porch.

Mom either saw or heard me coming up the stars. She met me at the door and said, "I'm almost ready."

"Mom, I haven't been here for a week, and you painted the porch! How did you find the time?"

My mother hugged me. Then she held my head in her hands and planted a kiss on both my cheeks and my forehead. She had done that for as long as I could remember, and it had become a ritual. It made me feel like a kid again and always made me smile.

"I didn't paint," my mother said. "Mr. Weaver said the place was looking a little shabby and needed a facelift."

Mr. Weaver was the resident of the big white house and my mother's landlord. Her apartment had benefited from several improvements since Mr. Weaver's wife died last year.

"Mom!" I teased, "I think Mr. Weaver's sweet on you."

"Well, he's wasting his time, as you know," my mother said, and winked at me.

My mother was almost fifty years old, but looked

less than forty. She was five feet two inches tall, like me, but probably weighed less than me. She had golden brown hair and her only wrinkles were the lines around her mouth and eyes, earned from constant smiling. She worked as a waitress and walked everywhere since she lived in town with easy access to her job, stores, dentists and doctors. It was a simple life, and she seemed happy with it.

I never knew of a man in my mother's life, except, of course, my grandfather. Mom didn't date when I was growing up, and I wondered if, like me, she had only a few dates in her life. Al was the only man I ever dated, but my mother never spoke about a man in her life.

Certainly, there had been a man or two in her life. I was proof of it, but my mother never talked about my father and, whenever I asked about him, my mother would say "someday." The last time I asked about him was on my wedding day. My mother's eyes had filled with tears and she said only, "It's your wedding day. Be happy."

I knew only that my mother had gotten pregnant twice. Once in her sophomore year of high school, but she lost the child in her fifth month of pregnancy and spent a year in therapy for depression. When she was twenty two years old, and still living with her parents, she got pregnant again.

I grew up in my grandparents' house in the city that was, at that time, known as East Detroit. Now it's called

Eastpointe. When I was ready to enroll in school, my mother moved us to the city of Richmond. She said she chose Richmond for its country atmosphere and the fact that all the schools, elementary through high school, were located in one area within the city. She found the garage apartment, two blocks from the schools, and I grew up walking to and from school each day with my mother.

One day I told her, "I can walk to school alone, Mom."

"I know, but I want to walk with you," my mother said.

"But it's embarrassing," I said, pleading with her. "Nobody walks the big girls to school."

"Oh, so you're a big girl now?" My mother folded her arms and looked at me.

I lost my patience and raised my voice. I had never done that before. "Yes! I'm a big girl! I got my period. I can walk myself to school. It's embarrassing to be walked to school by your mother!"

When my mother turned away with tears in her eyes, I regretted arguing with her. I took my mother's hand and held it to my cheek. "Don't cry, Mom. I'm so sorry. I didn't mean to make you cry. It's just that the other kids make fun of me. I'm sorry. Mom, please don't cry."

Thinking about it later that night, I realized that my mother was afraid to leave me alone. I didn't know why. But my mother was always there, watching out for me. So I continued to let her walk me to school, knowing that it was for her, and the other girls stopped teasing me. I would just smile if I saw them watching us, and they stopped teasing me. Maybe they were jealous. My mother was a beautiful woman.

After we moved to Richmond, Mom and I spent every weekend with my grandparents. My grandfather would pick us up on Saturday morning at 8 am in his old blue Ford pickup truck. Every Saturday, the conversation would be the same as Mom and I climbed into the truck after throwing our overnight bags in the back of it. My mother would complain, "Why do you need a truck, Dad? You don't haul anything. The car would be better."

"Aw, you're too practical," my grandfather would say and wink at me. "A man needs a truck!"

"Well, Mom's car would be more comfortable, and our stuff wouldn't have to go in the back of the truck if you brought the car."

"We always take the car when Grandma comes with us to bring you back on Sunday. You know that. But when I'm alone to pick you up on Saturday, I like to drive my truck. So let me be, and let me drive my truck," my grandfather would say.

My grandparents died in the car, going back to East Detroit after dropping us off on a Sunday afternoon. I was thirteen years old. The shock of their death, the emptiness without them in our lives, and the guilt my mother felt about insisting on a car ride every weekend haunted her.

After my grandparents' death, my mother started taking me to Saturday and Sunday riding lessons at a stable on the edge of town. It was a 15-minute walk from our apartment to Greenstone and the lessons filled our weekend. We walked together to the stable for my lessons at noon and mother watched me groom the lesson horse, tack up and take my lesson. After the lesson, she would help me untack and put the horse away, and during our walk home, we would discuss my lesson. Only heavy snow and ice storms kept us from our Saturdays and Sundays at Greenstone.

When I turned fourteen, I was offered a job at Greenstone and I was finally able to get away from my mother's watchful eyes.

First, I had to convince her to let me take the job. "Mom, you know you can trust Mrs. Greenstone. We've known her for a whole year. She raised three children. She's a good woman," I pleaded with my mother.

"I know, but there's the walk to the stable. I can't always go with you."

"Mom! I'll be walking down M-19. It's Main Street! The stable is just on the edge of town! What could go wrong?"

Mom looked at me and touched my hair. "Promise me you won't stop for anything? Talk to anyone? You will go straight to the stable and come straight hone?"

"I will go straight to the stable and straight home. I won't stop for anything and I won't talk to anyone.

Please, please, Mom, please let me take this job?"

Finally, my mother agreed. She stroked my cheek and said, "I know you have to grow up someday and I can't protect you forever. Just stay away from men. All men. Promise me that. Don't talk to men. Don't be alone with them. Promise me?"

I had never heard my mother talk about men. But I saw the worry in her eyes and agreed. "I won't talk to men and I won't be alone with a man. I promise."

My mother hugged me for a long time. When she finally released me, I saw that she had been crying while she hugged me.

"I love you," she said. "I always will, no matter what happens. Do you know that?"

I nodded. I didn't know what to say.

My mother turned away and began to prepare dinner. I watched her chop up lettuce for a salad and wondered what caused her to worry so much about men.

I didn't know many men. I had a couple of male teachers. Only one had made me nervous when his hand brushed up against my breast as we leaned over the lab table to examine my frog dissection in a biology class. But I moved away and nothing more happened. I couldn't tell if it had been intentional or an accident, but the teacher acted as if it had never happened. It was my only physical contact with a man other than my grandfather, and I assumed it was an accident.

In the end, I was allowed to take the job. I was paid

with a lease on a horse owned by the barn and weekly riding lessons. If I bathed and braided the school horses for their shows, I was allowed to go to the shows with my lease horse, all expenses paid. It was hard work, but I felt proud, and I learned a lot.

During my daily walk to the barn, I reviewed my schoolwork and during my walk home I re-lived my ride that day, trying to understand what didn't work and how I could improve on it the next day. I felt very mature.

When I got home, my mother would be cooking dinner. I loved our apartment above the garage. It was always filled with natural light, good smells, and fresh air. Flowers and baked goods were on the breakfast bar every day of the week. It was a happy, peaceful life.

Today was no different. I felt my shoulders loosen and relax the minute I walked in the door. When Mom grabbed me and planted the ritual kisses on my forehead and face, I smiled. When she released me, I showed her the flowers.

"Pretty!" she said. "There's a vase on the counter. I'll put on my shoes and be ready in a second. I can see you're dressed for the barn, so I won't waste any time." Mom headed to the back of the apartment.

"I'll go to the barn later today, Mom. I hope you don't mind that I'm dressed this way?" I called out to her. I didn't want to tell her that I had made a quick exit from my house and that my barn clothes were the easiest thing to put on in a hurry. I had no desire to ride. I just wanted to confront Cyra.

"Of course not! I never minded when you were younger, did I?" Mom called back.

I smiled and went to the kitchen area. I took the vase from the countertop, filled it with water, and tried to arrange the flowers. I gave up after they twice stubbornly returned to their original configuration. Then I sat down at the breakfast bar and warily looked around for Miss Priss.

As usual, my mother read my mind and called out, "I locked her in the bedroom!"

I let out a sigh of relief and picked up a magazine left on the breakfast bar. I was reading and chuckling over an article entitled "Six Ways to Get Your Man" when Mom emerged from the bedroom, glanced at the magazine and said, "Ain't that a hoot?"

"All that and a bag of chips!" I replied, laughing.

"Let's go to the new restaurant on Main Street," Mom suggested. "It's where the Town Clock was. Now it's called Ken's Country Kitchen. The new owner remodeled it, and the food is fantastic!"

"Okay. Sounds good."

It was a short walk to the restaurant, and I enjoyed the feel and sound of my shoes on the sidewalk. Mom and I had walked together for years, and we often played with the sounds of our footsteps, sometimes making a jazz-like sequence with them.

I thought about Layne's shoes and I wondered if she had gotten them fixed. No sneaky shoes for me. I enjoyed the sounds my feet made. I thought animals identified humans, even when they could not smell their presence, by the sound of their footsteps. I know Miss Priss did. Before my mother had started locking her in the bedroom when I came to visit, Miss Priss would be at the door, claws out. She was able to get in a few good swats before my mother could grab her "guard cat" and stow her away.

In a few minutes we arrived at the restaurant. It was newly decorated and smelled good. When we were seated, Pattu, the new owner, came to the table and welcomed us. She asked what we wanted to drink.

"Coffee!" Mom and I said at the same time and laughed.

After we ordered breakfast, Mom reached across the table and put her hand over mine. "How are you, dear?"

"I'm fine."

"No, you're not. Something's bothering you. You have that little vein standing out on your forehead. What's wrong?"

I rubbed my forehead and sighed. My mother knew me too well. "Mom, what would you do if you suddenly had doubts about your best friend?" I hoped my mother wouldn't ask about Al.

"Well, I would just ask them about it. Then watch them. You will know if they are lying or not by their body language."

I nodded. Mom was right.

After breakfast, I suggested a drive to the village of Almont for a little shopping. In Almont, we browsed in a quilt and antique shop and bought some jerky at the Country Smoke House. After that, we learned how to make soap and looked at metal artwork in another shop. Later, we had lunch at a restaurant in an old brick building that used to be a department store.

When I took Mom home, I hugged her and turned to leave. She grabbed my arm as I turned. "Just ask your friend about whatever is bothering you. Honesty is the best policy, you know."

I nodded. "I will," I said and gave her another hug.

It was 3:30 in the afternoon and I was driving in commuter traffic. I was beginning to feel tired from lack of sleep and worry, but I had to see Real. Just touching my horse and smelling him would give me the sense of peace that I had been missing since last night.

I turned off the road and onto the driveway of Centerline Farm. The sound of the driveway gravel under my car's tires seemed louder than ever before. And it seemed to take longer to get down the driveway and into the parking lot. I parked and turned off the engine and sat looking at the barn.

I saw Layne walk by the open door, bringing horses in from the paddocks. I visualized Real in his stall. He was probably eating hay and watching the other horses come in. I sat and watched him in my mind for a while.

Then I saw Cyra walk by the barn door and I was suddenly awake. My fingers tingled, and I sat straight up. I opened the car door, swung my legs out, touched the gravel with my boots and stood. I slammed the car door shut and marched to the barn and down the aisle toward Cyra.

Layne put Tempo in his stall and was closing the stall door when I called out, "Cyra! Do you have a minute?"

Layne's eyebrows shot up.

Cyra turned around and smiled at me. "Sure," she said.

Cyra was wearing a red tank top with black fringe that outlined her generous boobs and traveled around the top of her shoulders and ended at a point on her back. With her black breeches, black boots, and blackened eyes and mouth, all she needed was an elbow length pair of red gloves with black fringe to complete her female super-hero look. She approached me, strutting like a model on a runway, putting one foot directly in front of the other in a kind of rope walk that made her hips swing back and forth.

"What's up?" she said when she reached the place where I stood.

I hesitated. How could I be mad at Cyra, who was so open? Cyra never looked at anyone, except her horse, the way she was looking at me. It was a little unsettling. It disarmed me of my anger instantly.

"Um... can we talk in the observation room?" I could see Layne watching us, although she was trying to fold Tempo's fly sheet and arrange it on his stall door.

"Sure," Cyra said. "I could use a soda. Let's go!"

We walked up the stairs and into the observation room. I was relieved to see that no one was there. We were alone and we could talk freely.

While Cyra went to the soda machine, I stood at the observation room windows and watched Bonnie ride Bravo, her Grand Prix horse. Cyra came and stood by my side with two cans of soda. "Beautiful, huh?" she said, holding a sugar-free drink out to me.

I sighed and took the soda from her. "I wonder if I will ever learn to ride like that."

"Of course, you will!" Cyra said. "It took me a few years, but I'm almost there. You'll get there too."

"I hope you're right," I said and smiled. My anger was completely gone. How did Cyra do that? And she remembered that I was on a diet and bought me a sugar-free soda.

I sighed. "Layne and I went to the club last night. I saw you dance."

Cyra's eyes widened, and she smiled. "You did?" Then she laughed. "What did you think?"

"Um... it's quite an art form! And you're very good at it!"

Cyra laughed out loud and showed her perfect white teeth. "Thank you! But I've never heard it called an 'art form' before."

"Well, according to the internet, it is. I looked it up. Apparently, women have been dancing for men forever. Probably since the caveman." Why did I say that? I thought, I'm supposed to be giving her hell! What's wrong with me?

"How long did you stay?"

"Not long."

"Well, why didn't you say hi? Who went with you?"

"Layne. Something happened that upset me, so we left right after your dance."

"Oh. I'm sorry. It's just an act. I'm not a lesbian."

I shook my head. "It wasn't that."

Cyra just looked at me.

Okay, I thought. Here goes. I've got to get this out. I took a deep breath. "You went to the bar after your act, and you were talking to the owner and another man."

"Yeah. There was an 'incident' a couple of nights ago. They were asking me about it."

"That was my husband," I said, and looked deep into Cyra's eyes.

Cyra's eyes widened. She looked steadily at me. "No kidding? That's your husband?" Cyra frowned. "I thought I recognized him from somewhere, but, you know, in my profession... Now I remember. Your husband was here once, wasn't he, when you first came here?"

I nodded, watching Cyra's face.

"Then why didn't you come over?" Cyra asked, her eyes wide.

I realized that Cyra never blinked and never looked away as we were talking. Cyra was being honest. "I didn't know he was going to be there," I said. "He didn't know I was there. I saw him put some money in your string and I thought Jay was arranging a date with you. I panicked and Layne and I left."

"Oh." Cyra's blackened eyes searched my face. "I'm sorry. I understand. But I don't do dates. Jay asked him to come talk to us." Cyra continued in a low voice, "They were talking about the guy who got shot. My ex-boyfriend, Nic. You know, the one who was here, fighting with me at the barn? He used to work at the Club, but he quit and got crazy when I wouldn't see him anymore. You know, after he hit me."

Cyra sighed. "Nic's suing Jay. He came to the club and pulled out a gun. Demanded that Jay let him see me. Jay tried to get him to leave, and there was a scuffle. The gun went off and he was shot. With his own gun, the idiot! Nic's an idiot! Who would bring a gun to a nightclub and wave it around and act so stupid? Jay doesn't even have a gun! He has bouncers! Jay was trying to disarm him. Nic fought with him, and the gun went off. Now he's accusing Jay of shooting him."

I shook my head. "Nic can't be very bright." I laughed a little. "I'm glad no one got hurt but him. Serves him right."

Cyra looked at me. "So, that was your husband.

I didn't recognize him, but now I remember he was here. Before I met you. I think I met you that day."

"Yes, that was the day you fed Real some treats and introduced yourself."

"Jay said they went to school together. Grosse Pointe High School or something. So he asked him for advice and your husband asked me about Nic. I got a lot of grief from Jay for dating him." Cyra shook her head and sighed. "I don't know why he didn't fire me. What a mess!"

I let out a sigh, too. I was suddenly very tired.

Cyra put her hands on my shoulders and gave them a squeeze. "Hey, I'm sorry. I'm glad you told me." Then she hugged me.

I relaxed into Cyra's arms and hugged her back. Then I had to laugh. "That's the way my mom greeted me this morning, except she kissed me on the cheek too."

Cyra drew back and smiled, then kissed me on the cheek. "Wanna go for a ride?" she said.

"Don't you have to work?" I pointed at Cyra's shirt.

"No. I'm calling in sick. I have a friend who needs me." Cyra said and smiled again.

7 - MOVING UP

Cyra and I were getting ready for the second show of the season. I would be riding my last Second Level and my first Third Level tests at the next show, and I was excited.

Cyra was excited, and nervous too, because Bonnie had secretly entered her in a Grand Prix test. Cyra had read her classes and ride times on the internet that morning and went straight to Bonnie's office when she got to the barn.

I was standing in the office, talking to Bonnie and Layne, when Cyra peeked through the open door and entered.

"The show management made a mistake on my entry," she said. "They put me in a Grand Prix test. So, we need to scratch that when we get to the show grounds."

"That's no mistake," Bonnie told her. "I put you in. You're ready!"

Cyra looked at Bonnie for a minute. "Okay," she said and left without another word.

Layne stared at the door and said, "Well, a better response would have been thank you very much!"

Bonnie just smiled. "I've printed the semi-final list for Florida. Layne, will you post it outside?"

"Sure."

Bonnie always posted a semi-final list in July. In June, deposits had been made on housing and stabling fees. Sometimes things changed, and those who had made a deposit and couldn't go due to changing family circumstances, an injured horse or lack of funds could get a refund on their deposit.

Final payments for housing and stabling were due by July 1st. Housing and stabling could not be refunded and Bonnie posted a semi-final list then. Payment for training and coaching must be paid by September 1st. After September 1st, Bonnie would post the final list.

Bonnie handed Layne the seni-final list and I saw Cyra's name was on it.

"Is Irene okay with Cyra going now?" I asked.

Layne shook her head. "No, she will be livid when she sees this. I'll have to sit on her again."

I frowned and said, "Well, I'll see you guys later. I think I'll go see what's going on with Cyra." I moved toward the door.

At that moment, Irene opened the door and entered the room. The office was suddenly crowed and full of Irene's perfume.

Layne looked at her. Then she handed Irene the list for Florida. I leaned against the wall next to the door and waited for Irene to explode.

Irene said nothing. She put the list on Bonnie's desk and looked at Layne. "Let's go for lunch," she said.

Irene left the office, and Layne followed without

picking up the list.

Bonnie and I looked at each other and exhaled.

Bonnie shook her head. "You just never know," she said.

I laughed, relieved. "I'll post the list," I said.

"Thanks." Bonnie picked up her cell phone. "I've got a lesson in ten minutes. If you don't need anything, I'll make a quick call."

"No, I was just on my way out to see Cyra when Irene came in."

I didn't understand why Cyra was worried about riding Grand Prix. "Cheer up," I said when I found her in the tackroom. "You'll do fine!"

"It's not the test," Cyra said with a frown. "I'm okay with that. But Irene isn't showing Grand Prix yet. It just doesn't feel right."

"Oh. I see." I thought for a minute. "Cyra, are you worried that Irene will be angry?"

Cyra grabbed her saddle and put it on her hip. "No. I don't know why it bothers me so much, really." She thought for a minute and then said, "Well, I guess maybe it's because Irene taught me to ride when I was two and she was ten. It just doesn't feel right to be advancing before she does."

"Really? She taught you to ride? Tell me about it."

"Okay, I'm gonna clean my saddle. Grab yours if you want to clean it. I'll tell you about it while we clean tack."

"Good idea! I haven't cleaned tack since the last show. That's way too long." I grabbed my saddle, bridle, and girth.

Cyra and I took our tack outside and set everything down on a bench facing the parking lot. Then Cyra went to the shower stall and brought back a pail of warm water for us.

"Okay, sit," I said. "I want to hear how you learned to ride."

"There's not a lot to tell, really. I don't remember much because I was very young. I can remember being on a horse and sitting in front of my sister. As a baby, I had ridden in a 'cradle', you know, wrapped up and strapped to my mother's back when she went to work. Irene, or Ituha, let me ride with her when I was a toddler. I sat in front, and we rode to work. I sat in front when we came home. When I got older, she let me have the rein and guide the horse. When she left, I rode alone. That's all there was to it."

"Wow," I laughed. "And no helmet, I'm sure!"

Cyra smiled. "We never heard of such a thing. I'm sure people fell off horses back then too, but we weren't galloping all over the place or doing anything, really, just walking our horses to work. Sometimes they would see something frightening, like a coyote. Then we would shoot at it. Those horses were pretty bombproof!"

"You had a gun?"

"Our mother had a rifle. She always had it with her.

We went to work, and it was strapped to her horse. When we got to work, she hid it, but she always had one. Later on, after I left, she bought a small handgun. I think she liked it better than the rifle because she could hide it in her clothing."

"Why did your mom carry a gun? Was it just to scare off coyotes or wolves?"

"Maybe wolves with two legs. Wolves are pretty rare in Nevada, but coyotes are everywhere. I think my mother was afraid of the wolves that are men. She didn't feel at ease around men. If she had to talk to a man, she looked to the side, but never down. I was young, but I remember that." Cyra shook her head and sighed.

I was sorry I asked about Cyra's mom. Cyra had no one but a sister she couldn't confront. I reached over and touched her arm. "I am sorry. You aren't alone," I said. "I am your friend forever."

Cyra looked at me with her dark eyes. "I know," she said.

"May I ask you something else?"

Cyra nodded.

"What happened to make Irene leave? I know that you were very young, but do you remember?"

Cyra frowned. "No. One day, she was there. The next day she was gone. We went to work the next day, and I rode her pony. We called our horses 'ponies'. She didn't come back. Finally, I thought of her pony as mine."

"What did your mother say when Irene left?"

"Gaho said sometimes that happens with girls," Cyra said quietly. "She said, 'Sometimes girls go away.' Irene never came back until she came for me."

I thought a minute. "Cyra, what is Irene's Indian name? Ituha?"

Cyra nodded. "Ituha."

"What does Ituha mean?"

"It means Sturdy Oak."

"And what is your Indian name?"

Cyra looked at me with sad eyes. "My name is Enola."

"What does Enola mean?"

"Enola means Solitary Girl."

I suddenly realized I was holding my breath and quietly let it out. It was time to change the subject. I held up my girth. "Do you think I should get a new girth?"

8 - COLLUSIONS AND COLLISIONS

When I walked into the barn the next day, I was surprised to see Layne tacking up Parcel.

"Hi Layne. Where's Bonnie? I thought she always tacked up her own training horses?"

Layne frowned at me. "No. I'm riding Parcel. Irene just got here, and she's tired from shopping."

"Oh," I raised my eyebrows and laughed. "I didn't think anyone could get tired from shopping!"

Layne checked Parcel's girth and stroked his neck. "Horse shopping. She checked out a new horse this morning, and she's tired. She wants me to ride Parcel for her."

I teased Layne, hoping to get a smile out of her, "Oh, are you Irene's personal assistant or her new trainer?"

Layne frowned at me again and I thought, I'm talking too much. Maybe I drank too much coffee this morning. Or maybe Layne didn't drink enough.

"Actually, I'll be riding a lot of horses for Irene soon." Layne turned her attention back to Parcel, dropped the cross ties, removed his halter and bridled him.

That really confused me. "Wow. How does Bonnie feel about that? Isn't Irene Bonnie's client?"

Layne stopped moving abruptly. I could see her jaw tighten and her back get a little hunched. I had crossed the line.

"Oh, gosh, I'm sorry. It's none of my business! That just came out." I suddenly felt I was in the middle of trouble with Layne, Irene and Bonnie.

"It's alright," Layne said. "I have to talk to Bonnie later. There will be a lot of changes soon, since Irene is buying a farm."

"Oh. Bonnie still doesn't know?" I cringed. I was definitely asking too many questions. My mouth was going to get me in trouble.

"We haven't talked to her yet about our plans. We don't know when we're moving because we haven't found the right place yet and the place we get might need a lot of improvements."

"So, Bonnie doesn't know that you and Irene are buying a farm, and that Irene has become your client?" I was suddenly annoyed because Layne and Irene had changed everything without telling Bonnie about any of it. And I was annoyed with myself for not shutting up.

Layne shrugged. "I don't think Bonnie will care. Parcel will go to Florida and stay in training with Bonnie until they come back from Florida. I have to stay here to get our new place ready when we find the right place to buy. I always had to stay here, anyway. I never got to go to Florida," Layne grumbled.

I tried to make my words sound gentle. "Well, it's none of my business, but if it were me, I would have talked to her right away."

I had started the conversation, but I wished I hadn't. I knew I had stepped over a line and hoped that Irene and Layne would not hold a grudge.

"You're right. It's none of your business, but, for your information, I'm gonna tell Susan and Bonnie later today or tomorrow morning."

"Oh. Sorry." I turned away, intending to go to the tackroom, but Layne stopped me.

"I've been meaning to ask you, why have you and Cyra become so chummy lately? I see you two running off together all the time. Where do you go? Why do you want to hang around that piece of trash?"

I turned around and stared at Layne. I had never known Layne to say anything bad about Cyra before. I was shocked and speechless and didn't realize that my mouth was hanging open until Layne said, "Hey, shut your mouth! You know Cyra's a stripper and probably a whore!"

"Layne!" I said her name, but I couldn't think of anything more to say.

"So where do you two go? Got a little 'side' business going? I didn't pay much attention until Irene pointed it out to me. She says you are always going off with Cyra. Almost every afternoon! Where do you go?"

I suddenly felt violated. Was it Layne's and Irene's right to know my business? Did Layne have any right to question me about it?

I answered because I didn't know how to avoid it. "We go to lunch, we go on trail rides, and we used to go to school together on Mondays. Until Cyra got her associate's."

"School? What in the world were you two going to school for?"

"Pottery."

Layne just shook her head. "If you want my advice, stay away from Cyra. She's nothing. Irene said you shouldn't get too friendly with her."

I stiffened and stopped breathing. "Tell Irene that I don't need her to tell me how to choose my friends!"

"Suit yourself, but I think you're making a mistake. She's a good rider, but she's trash."

I took a deep breath. "Cyra has many good qualities and none of them are trash," I said and felt my voice rise as I continued, "She cares about her horse. She is sensitive to all kinds of beauty I never even thought about, and she doesn't say a bad word about anyone!" My voice had risen to almost a shout and my face felt hot. I turned and walked toward the tackroom.

The aisle wasn't long enough for me to regain my composure before I got to the tackroom door, and I marched in and almost collided with Irene, who was standing in the center of the room, arms folded across her chest. She was clearly angry, and I wondered if she had heard my conversation with Layne.

"Oh, excuse me. Sorry, I almost ran into you," I apologized and tried to move around her.

But Irene blocked my way. "I want to talk to you," she said.

"Okay." She heard me talking to Layne, I thought.

"You've gotten pretty tight with Cyra, and I think you're giving her big ideas!"

"What do you mean?" I said, frowning.

"She thinks she's going to Florida for the winter season! NO WAY! That can't happen!"

"Why not?" I was still angry, and Irene needed to get out of my way. "If she has the money and the time. She certainly has the horse and the talent!"

"Because she doesn't BELONG, that's why!"

"What makes you think that?"

"Because she's TRASH, that's why!"

"If SHE'S trash, then what are YOU?" I regretted it the minute I said it, but it was too late to take it back.

"And what do you mean by THAT?" Irene leaned into my space.

"Nothing." I dropped my head and tried to move past Irene.

But she blocked me. "WHAT do you mean by that?" she repeated.

I lowered my voice and tried to be calm. "Irene, just drop it. She's going. She has the money, the horse and the talent. She's going. End of story," I said with my head down. Inside, I was thinking, Irene, don't push me.

"Not if I can help it! Layne should be going, not HER!"

"Layne can't afford it, you know that, and, besides, who would take care of the farm and teach while Bonnie is gone?"

"That's not my problem. But I want YOU to talk that bitch out of it since you're the only one she talks to. You have to talk some sense into her!"

"I did. That's why she's going!" I snapped.

"What? This was all your idea? What do you have to gain by encouraging her to go where she doesn't belong?"

I looked at Irene and squared my shoulders. "If Cyra doesn't belong in Florida, then you don't either!"

"And what do you mean by THAT?"

"I think you know what I mean," I said quietly.

"What are you saying?"

"That you're the same as Cyra."

"What did you say?"

"You're the same as Cyra."

"How can you say that? We're not the same! She's a WHORE!"

"AND SO ARE YOU!"

Irene's face contorted and she slapped me so hard that tears sprang to my eyes and my head flew sideways.

I was furious. "Slap me again and I'll tell everyone who you are!" I yelled.

"What in the hell are you two fighting about?" Layne was standing in the doorway, having appeared silently on her "sneaky" shoes.

I turned to Layne. "I want you to leave. I have to talk to Irene about a personal matter."

Layne looked at Irene.

"Leave!" I yelled at Layne. She looked at me and saw that I wasn't kidding.

"Okay?" Layne looked at Irene again.

Irene waved her off. "Go," she said.

Layne shrugged and turned to leave.

But I didn't trust Layne and her "sneaky" shoes and said, "I want you to go to Bonnie's office and stay there until I come and get you."

Layne held up her hands. "Okay, okay!"

I stood in the doorway of the tackroom and watched Layne walk down the aisle past Parcel, who was on cross ties again, his halter placed over his bridle. I watched as Layne entered Bonnie and Susan's office and I watched as she closed the door behind her. Then I turned to Irene.

"It's time you stopped being such a bitch," I told her. Irene opened her mouth, but I held up my hand. "I know who you are, and I know about your past life, so if you don't want me to tell everyone who you are, you'd better start treating Cyra with respect. She's your sister and you've abused her enough already."

"What?" Irene squinted her eyes at me, her face contorted with anger.

"You don't know? You didn't recognize her?"

"What?" Irene repeated. "What did you say?"

I looked Irene in the eye. "She's your sister."

Irene's face became expressionless. All the blood drained away and her body slumped.

I nodded and stared at Irene.

"That can't be. I left her... that was years ago. Her name is Enola, not Cyra. I left her in Reno... "

"She was ten years old when you left her. Or I should say sold her?"

Irene sank back against the tackroom wall. "You know," she whispered.

"She told me. She told me all of it."

Irene looked at the floor and I continued, "She was given the name Cyra after you left her. She spent eight years in that prison for you!"

I paused to catch my breath, then continued. "She tracked you on the internet. Through your dressage show results. She learned that you trained with Bonnie, so she found Bonnie's farm and came here."

There was a long silence, and Irene lowered her head. I waited. After a while, Irene lifted her head. "How," Irene's voice was rough, and she cleared her throat, "how did she get to be such a good rider?"

"When she learned that you were a dressage rider, she talked her 'guardian' into letting her take dressage lessons. I can't imagine the price she had to pay for that favor!"

Irene had slumped back against the wall and put her arms around her waist, hugging herself. She stared at the back of the tackroom and started rocking from the waist up. Eventually she said, "She did all that, and she got free. She came here. She never told me."

"She said she came here to get even with you, but when she got here, and time went by, she changed. She didn't care anymore. So, she just stayed."

"Two years and she never said a word."

"I think she's happy just to be around you."

"She hates me."

"No, she doesn't," I told Irene. "She really doesn't."

I looked at Irene, but there was no reaction. "I think she loves you."

Still no reaction from Irene. "She's happy that you've become someone," I continued. "Of course, she would probably like it if you weren't so bitchy, but then she would have to be nice to you, and that would break down all the walls you two have built to protect yourselves."

Irene hung her head, and I watched as tears fell to the floor. Irene was crying silently, her body rocking against the wall.

Finally, I had to say something. "Irene, what's your Indian name?" Cyra had told me her name, and I remembered it and what it meant.

Irene looked up. "Ituha," she replied slowly.

"And what does it mean?"

"Sturdy Oak."

"Then be that."

Irene nodded slowly.

"I've got to go," I said and turned away from her.

"Wait," Irene said.

I stopped but did not turn around.

"Thank you," Irene said quietly.

"She loves you, Irene."

I walked out of the tackroom and gave Real and Chimmy a treat before leaving the barn. Maybe I wouldn't ride today. The atmosphere wasn't right. Real could use a day off, anyway.

I purposely did not go to the office for Layne. "Let her figure it out," I grumbled and went to my car.

I opened the door, got in my car and sat there for a few minutes, waiting for thoughts to come, but my mind was empty. I shook my head, started the car, and drove to the restaurant where my mother was working. I would have lunch and watch my mother at work. Then maybe I would go back to the barn and ride Real, after all. I missed him already.

Layne was taking a fly sheet off Tempo when I walked back into the barn that afternoon.

"Hi I. I'm gonna tell Susan and Bonnie about our plans now. You're right. It's time they knew."

I looked at Layne. "Does Irene know you're telling them today?"

"No, she left. Didn't even say goodbye. Come with me? After all, yo're the one who said I should tell them now. So, I'll do it."

"Okay," I said and thought, Why not? I'm already knee deep in this. At least I can let Cyra know what's going on.

Layne didn't knock. She just opened the office door and walked in. Susan looked up from her desk and put her cell phone down. Bonnie was going through a filing cabinet. She glanced up and smiled but went back to her work.

"Hey, can I interrupt you two for a minute?" Layne closed the office door behind us and shoved her hands into her breeches pockets.

"Sure," Bonnie looked up from her filing and turned to Layne. "What's up?"

Susan sat back in her chair and waited.

Layne looked at Bonnie and said, "Irene and I are buying a farm. Well, actually, we're looking at a few of them. We're gonna start our own business."

"That's great!" Bonnie grinned at her.

Susan knitted her hands together on the desktop. "And when will this happen?"

Layne turned to Susan. "I don't really know. We have to find the right place. I just thought it was only right to tell you now."

I looked down at the floor and coughed.

"Well, that's super!" Bonnie grinned at Layne.

Susan stood up from her desk. She walked around the desk and stood in front of Layne, who took a step back. "Let us know as soon as you find the farm, and congratulations!" Susan offered her hand to shake Layne's. Layne looked at it before putting her hand out to shake Susan's.

"Well, this calls for a celebration," Bonnie laughed. "But it will have to wait until you find the farm! In the meantime, we could have a small celebration over Mom's cheesecake in the observation room!"

"Sounds good," Susan said. "Let's go. I need a break, anyway."

"Wow. Okay," Layne seemed relieved that her news was well received.

Susan, Bonnie, Layne and I emerged from the office just as Cyra walked by the door. We almost collided with her.

"Oops! I'm sorry, Cyra!" Bonnie apologized. "We're kind of excited, but we shouldn't spill out the door like that! Sorry."

"No harm." Cyra said. "What's up?"

"Layne just told us that she and Irene have decided to go out on their own," Bonnie said. "They're buying a farm and starting their own business!"

"Really?" Cyra looked at Bonnie and Susan, but not at Layne.

"We will have an Open House. Everyone's invited." Layne was speaking mostly to Cyra. But Cyra did not respond.

"Great! We will all be there," Bonnie said. "We're gonna miss both of you around here!"

"Thanks." Layne looked at her watch. "Oops! No coffee for me. I have a lesson in ten minutes!" she said and headed down the aisle.

"Oh. Okay," Bonnie shrugged and turned to Susan and me, "Maybe we should finish those files and then get coffee and cheesecake? Is that okay?"

Susan nodded and spoke to me and Cyra. "Cheese cake and coffee are in the observation room. Help yourself."

"Thanks." I nodded at Susan and she and Bonnie went back into the office.

Cyra and I stood outside the closed office door.

Cyra dropped her head, sighed. Then she leaned back against the wall by the office door.

"Hey. Wanna go on a trail ride?" I asked.

Cyra looked up at me. "Yeah. Let's get out of here."

9 - THE REUNION

Cyra and I were grooming our horses and getting ready to practice for the next show. I was trying to find a good way to tell Cyra about my fight with Irene and that I revealed her identity. I wanted to tell her yesterday on our trail ride, but Cyra was so depressed that I couldn't. I thought it might crush her.

The problem kept me awake most of that night, but I couldn't think of a good way to tell her. I could not even think of a good way to start the conversation.

I was grooming Real in his stall as he ate hay and Cyra was grooming Chimmy on the crossties in the aisle. As I stood on tiptoe to brush the top of Real's hip, I saw Irene walking down the barn aisle toward Cyra.

Her walk was slower than normal. She still had a sexy sway to her walk. It was hard to walk any other way with her long legs. But her walk looked hesitant as she approached Cyra, who was watching her out of the corner of her eye as she brushed Chimmy.

I dropped down and watched the two women from behind Real's hip, and thought, "Irene looks so timid, if Cyra growls at her, she'll probably run away."

But Cyra kept brushing, and Irene kept walking. Finally, she was standing by Cyra. I tried to keep quiet because Irene didn't know I was in Real's stall. I didn't want to interrupt what was happening between the sisters. Of course, Cyra knew I was in Real's stall and maybe that was a comfort to her.

Irene stood by Cyra for a few moments. I saw her hand twitch a little as if it wanted to touch Cyra, but she got control of it and balled it into a fist. "Enola," she whispered with an inflection I had never heard before.

Cyra dropped her head.

Irene had tears streaming from her eyes. "Enola," she whispered again.

Cyra put her arms over Chimmy's back and leaned into Chimmy's side. I could see that her body was shaking and I thought Cyra might be crying too, but she threw her head back and emitted a deep, aching moan that escalated into a scream: "Ah-a-a-ahhhhhh!"

Chimmy startled and jumped away two steps. I twitched and Real threw his head up.

Cyra turned to Irene, still moaning, and started pounding her sister with her fists. Irene leaned into Cyra and let her continue until she stopped, exhausted. Then she wrapped her arms around Cyra and cried silently, her face an almost expressionless mask with tears running down the cheeks. Cyra was crying too, but with her mouth frozen open in anguish.

At that moment, Layne walked around the corner of the aisle, halted and stared at the two women. I held my breath and waited for Layne to spoil everything with an unkind remark, but Layne turned abruptly and left. Irene and Cyra had not seen her or heard her entrance and exit.

I remained in the stall behind Real. After a while, Cyra took Chimmy off the crossties without saying a word and put her in her stall next to Real. Then she turned to Irene. Irene took her hand, and the two women left the barn.

I emerged from Real's stall and took a deep breath. Suddenly, Layne was beside me, and I jumped in surprise.

"Sorry, I didn't mean to scare you."

I looked down at Layne's feet. She was wearing her shoes with the rubber soles. "You shouldn't sneak up on people! I thought you were getting taps or something put on those?"

"I haven't done it yet. Tomorrow's my day off. I'll try to do it then. Sorry." Layne shifted on her feet. "So, what was that all about? They're lovers now?"

I frowned at Layne.

"I saw you in the stall, hiding behind Real."

"I wasn't hiding. It's just that Irene didn't know I was there, and she had something to say to Cyra that was very personal. I didn't think I should let her know I was there. I didn't want to ruin anything."

"What would she say to Cyra other than kiss my ass? She tells her that all the time!"

I narrowed my eyes at Layne. "She said, you are my sister. She called Cyra by her real name - Enola."

Layne blinked and stared at me. Finally, she

said, "What?"

I looked at Layne but said nothing.

"You're serious?" Layne asked.

I nodded slowly.

10 - CHANGES

I gave Real a treat and stroked his neck. I hadn't seen or heard from Cyra in three days. I sighed. Things had changed. I missed Cyra. The barn seemed empty. Irene and Cyra seemed to have disappeared. They had been gone for almost two weeks.

Layne hadn't been around much either.

"Good morning, Marsha!" Susan called out.

I turned in the direction of Susan's voice and smiled. "Good morning, Susan. I was just thinking that the barn seemed empty. It's good to see you."

"It is a little empty, isn't it? Well, change can be like that. It makes life either too busy or too empty."

I could only nod.

"Anyway," Susan continued, "Bonnie is in the office. She asked if you had a minute?"

"Sure," I nodded again.

"Good. I'm on my way to the feed store. See you later," and Susan was gone.

"Bye," I said to Susan's retreating back, but I knew she hadn't heard me.

I closed Real's stall door and left him to finish his hay, then walked to the office, tapped on the half open door and entered without waiting for an answer.

Bonnie was sitting at the desk when I entered. She

motioned me to one of the chairs in front of the desk and I sat down.

Bonnie got right to the point. "I, I want you to forget about Second Level."

I opened my mouth, but no words came out. I felt my shoulders drop. Evidently, I hadn't done well enough at Second Level, in Bonnie's opinion, even though my scores had all been above 65% and one was a 72%.

"Don't look so glum," Bonnie said. "You're doing great! I want you to start showing at Third level and schooling Fourth. That is, unless you want to qualify for Regionals at Second Level? Then, you should stay in Second to qualify, of course."

"Uh, no. I don't really care about qualifying."

"Great! You're ready to advance, and I would like to take over your training, if that's okay with you?"

"Oh, yes!" I breathed out in relief. "So, you think I'm ready to move up?" I winced. She had just said that.

"Without a doubt," Bonnie said with a smile.

"Great! And I would love to be trained by you, but I thought you only worked with FEI riders?"

"In the past, yes. But, until I find a replacement for Layne, my mother will teach students, beginner through First Level and I will teach students above First Level."

"Oh. Is Layne leaving? I thought that wouldn't happen until next winter."

"Layne told me this morning that she wants to make the move immediately. I don't know what the hurry is. I thought she and Irene were taking their time to find the right farm, but maybe they found it. So, anyway, Layne said I should start making plans, and I thought I would start working with you this week, if that's okay with you?"

"Well, yes, and thank you for your confidence in me!" I smiled at Bonnie. Then my smile faded. "Are you okay with Layne leaving? What about your trip to Florida?"

"I'm fine with it! Layne had to move on someday. I just thought she would wait until she got her gold medal. But it's okay with me. And I have enough time to look for a new barn manager and assistant trainer to help Mom while I'm in Florida. Hopefully, I will find one that will stay and take Layne's place."

"Oh," I said and then got annoyed with myself. It seemed like all I could say was, "Oh."

"And, just so you know, most lesson times will stay the same, but a couple might change. I'll have a new schedule posted on the office door tomorrow."

"Well, okay, I'm looking forward to it," I said and stood up. "I know you're busy, so is that all?"

Bonnie stood and smiled gratefully. "Yes, thank you. I'll see you in your lesson tomorrow."

Closing the office door, I let out a breath I didn't know I had been holding. I was sad, lonely and amazed, all at the same time. Layne and Irene would be leaving.

That meant Cyra would leave, too. I would be showing at Third Level and schooling Fourth and doing it with Bonnie. The news was exciting, but I felt empty and sad. I had no one to share it with.

The next day, I was getting ready for my first lesson with Bonnie and thinking about braiding Real's mane when Cyra and Irene walked into the barn, laughing.

They walked up to me, and I smiled. I had never seen either of them so relaxed and happy.

Cyra said, "Hey, congratulations! I hear you're taking lessons with Bonnie now and that you'll be showing Third and schooling Fourth Level. Bonnie told me this morning when I paid my board."

"Yes, I heard that too," I said, laughing.

"That's great." Irene smiled at me.

It had been a week since Cyra and Irene were reunited and I knew my relationship with Cyra had changed forever. Now Irene was Cyra's best friend. I knew it should be that way. But I missed Cyra's company.

Now Irene was smiling or laughing and Cyra had a serenity about her that I knew had been missing for years. She didn't wear heavy makeup or piercings to the barn anymore and I wondered if she was still working.

Layne was back in the barn again but was looking worse as each day passed. I thought she looked like she was losing sleep, and one afternoon, I thought she had been drinking. She was probably working herself to exhaustion, running the new barn and working at Centerline too. I wanted to congratulate her on the upcoming move to her new farm, but she didn't hang around the barn much and didn't seem in the mood for conversation. She was still teaching some of the lessons, but she seemed to be in a hurry and left right after teaching them.

Thinking about Layne reminded me that I hadn't congratulated Irene on her new business venture with Layne. "And I heard congratulations are in order for you too," I said to Irene.

"Oh? Why?"

"I heard that you and Layne bought a farm and will be moving soon. Congratulations!"

"No, I haven't bought a farm. I haven't really thought about it lately." Irene shrugged and looked at Cyra.

"Oh," was all I could say. I was confused. Why had Bonnie taken over most of the lessons if Layne and Irene hadn't bought a farm? And why was Layne gone most of the time? I shrugged it off. Maybe she had found another investor. Maybe her husband? Maybe she was busy fixing up her new barn.

Things had changed for me at home, too. Al was working in Michigan again and was home early every night, so my days were filled with riding, shopping for dinner, and spending time with Al. I stopped thinking that he might be having an affair because he was spending every night at home with me. I finally talked about it one night when we sat down for dinner.

"Al," I said as I watched him cut into his steak, "I was beginning to think that you had found someone else."

Al looked up. "What?"

"You know, you were spending so much time in Texas then Philadelphia, New York and New Jersey. And, when you were home, you spent long hours away. You came home late at night, exhausted and just went to bed. So, I wondered."

Al put his fork down. He reached across the table and put his hand on mine. "Sometimes my work is like that," he said. "Sometimes I'm so busy I don't have time to come home and pack my bags. That's why I have suits and overnight bags at the office. That thing in Texas took me away for quite a while, but our client was acquitted. After that, it was cases in Philly, New York and Jersey. When we have a big case, our team meets almost every night until midnight, sometimes later. Right now, we're dealing with smaller cases, but when another big one comes up, I'll be really busy again." Al squeezed my hand.

"I know." I hung my head. "And I don't mean to be a whining wife, but I missed you."

Al took my chin in his hand and forced me to look at him. "I love you. Don't forget that. I love you, and I love my work. In this profession, you can't punch a clock 9 to 5. I need you to understand that. And when clients get in trouble, my life belongs to them for a while. That's just how it is. I'm sorry I have to be away so much. I really am. But don't ever think I have any other women in my life besides you and Lady Law!"

I smiled at that and Al got up and pulled me from the table.

"Al! What are you doing?"

Al picked me up and carried me to the bedroom. "Dinner can wait," he said.

11 - CYRA IS LATE

I was walking Real out to his paddock when I saw Chimmy grazing at the side of the outdoor arena, wearing Cyra's handmade bridle. The single rein was trailing between her legs as she grazed. I put Real in his paddock and went to get Chimmy, then brought her inside, put her in her stall and removed the bridle.

Confused, I hung the bridle on the halter hook by her stall door. Then I walked to the office to find Layne or Bonnie. I knocked on the door, peeked in and saw Layne standing by the file cabinet. She turned and frowned at me. Bonnie was standing behind the desk, her arms folded.

I hesitated at the door. It was obvious that I had come at a bad time and interrupted something. But Bonnie waved me in. "Hi, Marsha. Do you need something?"

"Sorry. I just wanted to tell you that I found Chimmy loose outside. She was grazing by the outdoor arena. I put her in her stall."

"What?" Bonnie said. She looked at Layne. "Who put Chimmy out today?"

"Cyra. She said she was going for a trail ride this morning and she would put her out after."

Bonnie looked at her watch. "Well, it's not morning

now. It's 3:30."

Layne folded her arms at her waist. "Cyra probably put her out and left. Probably forgot to latch the gate."

"No," I said, "something isn't right. Cyra wouldn't forget something like latching a gate and Chimmy was wearing her handmade bridle."

"What?" Bonnie was confused too.

"I'll find the barn help and see if they know anything," I told her.

"Thanks. Keep me posted?" Bonnie asked.

"Okay." I backed out of the office and closed the door.

Standing outside the office, I was anxious and couldn't decide which way to go. Then I saw Irene cross the aisle and enter the tack room. I headed for the tack room.

"Irene, have you seen Cyra or talked to her today?"

Irene turned and smiled at me. "No, I haven't yet, but we're having dinner at my house. She's supposed to meet me here. I want to show her my new bridle." Irene picked up a bridle with a double row of crystals on the browband and held it out to me.

"Very nice!" I said and touched the soft leather of the bridle. "Okay. Maybe she went shopping. Maybe she went to buy a bottle of wine for your dinner." I smiled, then frowned. "But she left her bridle on Chimmy and I found Chimmy grazing outside by the arena."

"Really?" Irene frowned.

"Yes. Chimmy was loose. I found her loose by the outdoor arena. Layne thinks Cyra put her out and forgot to close the gate." I took a deep breath. "Layne said Cyra went for a trail ride this morning, but I found Chimmy outside with her bridle on. So, none of it makes sense." I frowned.

"That doesn't sound like Cyra! Maybe she handed her off to one of the working students, and they put her out with the bridle on. They probably didn't know it was a bridle!" Irene said and laughed. "It ooks like a weird halter with a lead attached."

That made sense. "Maybe that's what happened. And if she's having dinner at your house, and wanted to run an errand first, she was probably in a hurry and just handed her off. You're probably right."

Irene nodded. "That's right," she agreed. "Hey, why don't you join us for dinner?"

"Oh, I couldn't. It's your family's dinner."

"Not really." Irene insisted. "It's just me, Joey and Cyra. If Al is in town, bring him, too. Joey will enjoy having another man around!"

"Are you sure? We don't want to intrude."

"It's just an informal dinner. We're having Cornish game hens. Joey is cooking, and he always makes too much food!" Irene laughed.

I smiled. "That sounds wonderful. I'll call Al. What time is dinner?"

"Five sharp, so get on it!" Irene teased.

As I waited for Al to answer my call, I thought about

how much Irene had changed since she and Cyra were reunited. She seemed like a totally different person. It was getting hard to remember the old Irene.

I had to leave a message on Al's cell phone, but he called me back a few minutes later.

"Hi, Hon. I'm wrapping things up here. Dinner sounds great! I've always wanted to meet Joey. I've heard a lot about him."

"Dinner is at 5 o'clock."

"Humm... would it be okay if I meet you at their house? I still have a couple of things to do here, and I could make it by five o'clock that way."

"I'm putting you on speaker," I said, nodding yes to Irene.

Irene spoke up, "Hi Al, This is Irene."

"Hi Irene," Al said. "I hear we're invited to dinner?"

"You bet!" Irene laughed.

"Do you mind if I go directly to your house? I'm trying to wrap things up at work."

"That's perfect," Irene replied. "Just go north on Moravian Drive, past Metro Parkway, and you will see a gated community on the left. Push the button and let the gatekeeper know who you are, and he will open the gate. Our house is the third on the right. See you at five!"

I looked at my riding breeches. "Irene, I don't have time to go home and change, so I'll have to clean up in the barn washroom and go to your house in my riding clothes, if that's okay."

"No problem," Irene smiled at me. "We are very informal at home," she said.

Relieved, I decided to wipe down my saddle before cleaning myself up.

At 4:15. Irene said, "Cyra should be here any minute."

But at 4:30, Irene started getting impatient. "Cyra should be here by now," she said.

"Maybe she decided to go directly to your house?"

"No, we specifically decided to leave from the barn. I said I would drive, and she would spend the night." Irene smiled at me. "She spends the night with me and Joey a lot. We have so much to talk about and plans to make."

I smiled because Irene looked happy, but I felt sad. I missed Cyra and the time we used to spend together.

At 4;40 Irene called Cyra's cell phone, but it went to voicemail. Irene hesitated, then said, "Enola, please call me back. It's getting late. Marsha and I are at the barn waiting for you. Where are you?" Irene put her cell phone in her pocket and folded her arms around her waist. She was frowning and looking at the barn door.

"She's probably caught in traffic," I said. "There is a lot of road construction going on. Maybe she didn't hear the phone, or her signal might be weak."

Irene nodded. "You're probably right."

At 4:45, Irene called Cyra's cell phone again, but there was no answer. She left a second message. "Now

I'm really starting to worry!" she said. Then she called Joey and explained that we were delayed, waiting for Cyra.

At the same time, I called Al. He was already at Joey and Irene's house. "I'm standing next to Joey and I heard that Cyra is late? 45 minutes late and no word from her?"

I walked a few feet away from Irene. "Yes, and I found her horse loose and bridled!" I kept my voice low so Irene wouldn't hear.

"And now you tell me you found her horse loose at the barn? Something isn't right," Al said. "I think we should go to the barn."

I could hear Al talking to Joey. Then he came back to me. "I, Joey and I will be there soon. We will drive separately, but we will both be there."

When Al and Joey walked into the barn, they found Irene and me standing in the middle of the barn aisle, talking to Layne and Bonnie. Joey walked over to Irene and stood by her.

"When was the last time anyone saw Cyra?" Al asked all of us.

"No one saw her but Layne. The working students and some of the boarders got here after nine, but no one saw her," Bonnie said.

Layne frowned. "I saw her this morning. She was going on a trail ride. I didn't see her after that."

"Something's wrong!" Irene hugged herself. Joey

put his arm around her.

"Do you think she just forgot?" Layne asked.

Irene looked at Layne, then shook her head. "No, we talked about this on Tuesday and again yesterday. She wouldn't forget, anyway." Irene started to rock back and forth with Joey's arm around her.

"Al," I touched my husband's arm, "can I talk to you outside?" Al nodded and followed me out the barn door to the patio.

"Let's walk," I said.

We walked across the parking lot in silence. I didn't know where I was going, but I had to move. We walked through the parking lot and toward to line of horse trailers. Suddenly I stopped. "Al! That's her car!" I pointed, "There!" The little blue sedan Cyra owned was parked next to the Centerline Farm horse trailers.

Al walked toward the car, and I followed. "Is she in the back? Is she asleep in the back? She did that sometimes. She would sleep in her car after work so we could ride together in the mornings."

Al got to the car before me. "She's not in the car," he said.

Then he walked to the front of the car. He put his hands on the hood of the car. "It's cold," he said.

I couldn't say anything. I just looked at Al.

"Not a good sign," Al said and pulled out his cell phone. He punched in a number.

"Who are you calling?"

Al held up a finger. "Hello," he said. "My name's

Alton Myers. I would like to report a missing person." Then he gave Cyra's name, asked me her age and the address of the stable. "Yes. Yes, I understand. No, we don't have any evidence of that. Yes. Well, can you send someone out, anyway? Okay. Thank you."

"Al, do you really think that's necessary? She's only an hour late."

"She didn't call, she doesn't answer her cell phone, her car has been here for a long time, and it's out of character for her to be late. It's never too early to report a missing person. If she is truly missing, and it appears that she is, time is of the essence. She might have been abducted while she was riding on the trail this morning."

I gasped, then stifled it. The ex-boyfriend. Of course. He was probably out on bail and very angry.

Al and I went back inside the barn, where Irene and Joey were talking to Layne and Bonnie.

Bonnie asked Layne, "You know her best, Layne. Has she ever done anything like this before?"

Layne had been staring at the floor. She jerked her head up, and her eyes were large and glassy. She shook her head.

Irene spoke up, "She's always been on time when we've gone out to lunch or rode together, but I haven't done a lot with her until recently." I noticed that Irene was still hugging herself and rocking.

"I called the police. They're sending an officer out." Al said.

Layne looked up suddenly. "Why?" she said.

"Cyra's car is in the parking lot. The engine is cold. It's a warm day, and the engine is cold. She hasn't left any messages, and she doesn't answer her cell phone. Something's not right."

"Oh." Layne dropped her head.

Irene's face was bloodless. "Her car is... I didn't see it earlier. It's cold?"

Joey tightened his arm around Irene's hunched shoulders and I went to stand on her other side.

"It is parked behind the horse trailers. You wouldn't have seen it," I told her quietly.

"I didn't see it there." Irene was crying and confused.

Joey pulled Irene into his arms.

I'll wait outside until the police arrive," Al said. "Why don't you all wait in Susan's office?"

I shook my head. "I'm going with you."

Fifteen minutes later, a police cruiser pulled up to the barn and two officers stepped out. "Officer White," the larger man indicated himself, "and Officer Krause," he said, indicating the other man.

"Thank you for coming," Al said, and told them about Cyra's unexplained absence and the discovery of her cold car.

"All I can do right now is record her as missing and then we wait," Officer White said. "You have to understand that she is an adult and, unless there is evidence of foul play, or if the person was in danger due to a medical problem, we can't investigate more aggressively. People have a right to their privacy. But if you can find any evidence of a medical problem or foul play, we can proceed."

Al looked at me. "Did Cyra have any medical problems? Diabetic? Epileptic? Anything?"

"No." I shook my head.

Officer White pulled out a notebook. "I'll take her name and some other information, but we can't begin a search until 24 hours have passed since she was last seen."

Al nodded, and I gave Officer White Cyra's name, address and phone number.

"The last person to see her was Layne, one of the trainers. She saw her this morning," I added.

Officer White nodded, wrote in his notebook, and closed it. "Alright. You have our number. Call us if she doesn't show up by tomorrow morning."

Al and I watched the officers get into their car and drove away.

I frowned. "I don't understand why they came!"

"They came because I asked them to," Al explained patiently. He stepped forward and drew me into his arms. I sighed and relaxed in his embrace.

"If Cyra were a minor, they could search for her now. But she is an adult without medical problems and we have no evidence of foul play, so they have to wait at least 24 hours. Michigan law." Al stroked my hair.

I drew back and looked at Al. "The only thing I can think is that maybe her ex-boyfriend met her here and took her somewhere." I frowned. "That's got to be it. He's keeping her against her will somewhere. He must have grabbed her outside. I found her horse, loose in the back and bridled." I grabbed Al's arm. "He's got her! We've got to find him!"

"Calm down. That's not possible," Al said.

"Why? It must be him! It's got to be him!" I looked at Al.

"No. He's still in jail for assaulting Jay. I checked twenty minutes ago. No bail was posted."

"Oh," I searched Al's face, remembering that Jay was his childhood friend. "Is Jay in jail?"

"No," Al said and smiled, "he has a good lawyer."

Al and I went back to the office. Bonnie was talking to Layne and Susan while Irene leaned against the wall and her husband. Bonnie turned to us.

"Well?" she asked.

"He can't do anything except record it," I said. "But Cyra's car is in the parking lot. By the horse trailers. The engine is cold. That must mean something?"

Bonnie thought about that for a minute, then looked at Layne and back to me. "Okay," she said, "maybe the police can't do anything yet, but we can. The last time Cyra was seen by anyone, as far as we can tell, was Layne. Layne, you said she was going on a trail ride. Where was she going? Out to state land? Did she tell you?"

Layne shrugged. "Just on a trail ride."

"Okay. Let's get some horses and go out back. Maybe we can track her. If Chimmy was loose, maybe it wasn't because the pasture gate was left open." Bonnie looked at me. "Maybe Cyra is out there. Maybe she had an accident or was abducted while she was riding on state land. Anyway, we've got to do something. Let's get our horses and search the trails. Layne, you and Marsha come with me. Irene, you stay with the men."

"No! I'm coming too!" Irene said, her eyes flashing.

"Okay. You can take Trooper. I'll take Bravo. Layne will take Rodney. Marsha?" Bonnie hesitated and looked at me.

"What?"

"Will you take Chimmy?"

My eyes widened. Then I understood. "Yes." I said.

"I was just thinking it might help," Bonnie said. "Let Chimmy lead us. If she will."

I nodded.

By that time it was 6 pm, but it was the middle of summer and it wouldn't start to get dark until around 8 pm. We saddled up quickly, glad to have something to do, and assembled at the back door of the barn. Without saying anything, Bonnie turned her horse, and I walked alongside her with Chimmy. Layne and Irene followed behind us.

It seemed to take forever to get to the meadow. We were going slow enough to check every part of the trail and to watch Chimmy's reactions.

After a half hour of slow moving, I was starting to think that we were wasting our time. Maybe Cyra brought Chimmy back to the barn, let her graze, then got distracted and left. Or handed her off to a working student. Or was abducted. I shook myself and stopped thinking.

Eventually, we crossed the stream and entered the meadow. Halfway across the meadow, a deer jumped up and fled into the woods, startling us and three of the horses. But there was no reaction from Chimmy. She seemed to be half asleep.

We crossed the little stream, and I resisted the impulse to jump off Chimmy and grab a river rock. Then we entered the woods. We were still walking slowly, but at that point, Chimmy grew noticeably reluctant to put one foot in front of the other. About 100 feet before we got to the clearing with the statue of the Indian girl, Chimmy stopped and began to tremble. Bonnie moved Bravo closer to Chimmy and tugged on her bridle. She urged Bravo to walk and Chimmy followed.

When we got within 50 feet of the clearing, we could see Cyra's body laying by the statue. It was obvious, even from a distance, that she was either unconscious or dead. Blood had coagulated on her face and soaked into the ground around her head.

Bonnie and I saw her first, then Irene and Layne saw her. Irene gasped, jumped off her horse, and ran to cover Cyra's body with her own. Layne stared at the scene wide-eyed.

Bonnie started to get down from her horse, but I grabbed her arm. "No," I said.

Bonnie looked at me, confused.

"Don't touch anything," I said and pulled out my cell phone. I speed-dialed Al. When he answered, I told him, "Call the Officers. Ask them to come back. We found her."

I listened a minute, then said, "On state land. There is a road that goes through. Tell the police she is about 1/2 mile north of the creek behind Centerline Farm. We will send a rider to the road to meet them.'

Bonnie raised her hand slightly, telling me she would go to meet them.

"They might have to walk in. I don't know. But Bonnie will meet them and guide them here. It's not far from the road."

"What is her condition?" Al asked.

I had a lump in my throat, but I took a deep breath and said, "We don't know if she's unconscious or worse, but there is a lot of blood and we need an ambulance."

Al didn't ask any more questions. "Okay," he said. "I'll call you back."

Then Bonnie spoke: "What are you thinking?"

I could hear Irene sobbing. "Nothing," I said. "Just don't touch anything."

Bonnie nodded.

I said, "Irene?"

Irene wouldn't look up, but she moaned so I knew she heard me. "Is she breathing?"

Irene slowly shook her head.

I said, "Irene, we need to leave her as we found her so the police can figure out what happened, okay?"

There was no answer from Irene. I watched as she slowly rose to her knees and stroked Cyra's back. With a shock, I saw that her pose mirrored the statue of the Indian girl and the fawn.

I shook myself and said, "Irene, please go back to the barn with Layne and wait for us?"

Irene rose to her feet and I could see that her clothes had blood on them. Cyra's blood. She slowly walked to her horse and picked up the reins.

Layne turned Rodney around and walked him. Irene followed behind, her head down, walking beside Trooper. Layne stopped Rodney, jumped off him, and walked beside Irene.

Bonnie rode Bravo through the woods to the state road to wait for Al and the police, leaving me alone with Cyra's body. I dropped my eyes and stroked Chimmy's neck. I wanted to jump off Chimmy and run to Cyra, but my body felt like cement, and I knew I shouldn't disturb the area.

I didn't look up again until Al touched my leg.

I startled and slid off Chimmy into Al's arms. I had the reins to Chimmy's bridle clutched tightly in my hands and Bonnie pried open my fist and took them.

"I'll take her back," she said quietly.

Policemen came and taped off the area. Then two detectives, a photographer, and the ambulance crew arrived. A member of the crew examined Cyra's body and shook his head. After that, the position of Cyra's body was outlined in chalk, photographs were taken, items were put in plastic bags, and the ambulance crew was allowed to take Cyra's body away.

I stared at the white chalk lines and blood. "Why are they doing that?"

"It's an unexplained death," Al said, rubbing my back.

"What do you mean?"

"Nothing," Al said. "It's just unexplained. They need to analyze the scene and find out what happened."

"Oh." I put my head back on Al's chest. I couldn't breathe and I couldn't cry. My legs felt like sticks of wood.

One of the detectives said to no one in particular, "It's gonna be dark soon. Let's get a tent and some lights over here."

Soon, a large tent was erected over the statue and the surrounding area and lights were hung. A portable generator was started up to power the lights, and the investigation continued. Signs were hung at the entrance to the state land and on both ends of the trail, saying that the area was closed until the police investigation was complete.

After watching the detectives for another half hour,

Al gently massaged my shoulder and said, "Let's go back to the barn? Okay?"

I nodded, but couldn't speak.

When we arrived at the barn, we found Officer White in the office with Bonnie, Susan, Joey, Irene and Layne. Joey had his arm around Irene and Layne was leaning against the filing cabinet, arms folded, staring at the floor.

Joey looked up when we walked into the room. He walked over to us and said quietly, "I'm gonna ask Officer White if I can take Irene home."

Al nodded. "Layne probably would like to go home, too."

Joey turned to Officer White. "Officer, I'd like to take my wife home. Today's been hard on her."

"That's fine," Officer White said. "I just need your address and phone number."

After giving the information to Officer White, Joey put his arm around Irene and said, "Let's go home."

Layne jerked her head up and unfolded her arms. She walked over to Officer White.

"You probably want to leave too," he said. I'll need to see your license or ID."

Layne snatched her purse off Bonnie's desk and pulled her wallet out of it.

Officer White copied the information he needed from her driver's license. "And I need a number where you can be reached."

Layne shifted on her feet. "Here or home?"

"Both."

Layne sighed and gave him the numbers.

Joey turned to Layne and touched her shoulder. She flinched.

"Sorry," Joey said and lowered his hand. "Do you want us to drive you home?"

Layne shook her head. "No. I have my car." And a second later she added, "Thanks."

Joey turned back to Irene. He took her hand, and nodding to Al and me, led her out of the office.

Al and I stayed in the office with Bonnie, Susan and Officer White. The officer thumbed through his notebook and sighed. "I will need your phone number," he said, looking at Susan.

Susan gave him the office and her cell number.

"I think that's all I need for now. I'll be in touch," he said and nodded to Al and I as he left the office.

Bonnie sighed and looked at us. "How sad."

"Yes," I said. "I think we will go home now, if you're okay."

"Yes, go. Go home. Get some rest."

We drove home, Al in his car, and I followed Al in mine. I don't remember the drive home. All I remember is that the trip seemed to take forever. When we got there and parked in the garage, Al walked around his car and helped me out of mine. He took me in his arms and held me for a long time. Finally, we parted and walked into the house, holding hands.

Al undressed me and put my nightgown on. I felt like a child, but I couldn't function. Then he picked me up and carried me to the bedroom. I don't remember falling asleep.

12 - WHAT HAPPENED?

After Al and I left the barn, Susan and Bonnie were alone in the office. Susan shook her head and sighed. "We shouldn't talk to the boarders about this,"

"They will be asking questions, Mom."

"I know. We don't know anything, really." Susan frowned. "All we know is that Cyra is gone. We don't know why. And we don't want gossip and rumors to start."

"I know. But shouldn't we call the boarders and tell them what we do know? And ask them to be patient? Don't they have a right to know as much as we do?"

Susan sighed again. "You're right. Okay. But it's getting late. I'll call half of them, and you call the other half."

"Just tell them that Cyra's body was found by the statue. Tell them we don't know what happened, but the police are investigating her death, and that's all we know," Bonnie said.

"You're right. Okay."

The next day at the barn was difficult. Some of the boarders hugged each other and talked about how empty the barn felt. Others theorized about what might have happened. Some even seemed to be angry with

Cyra. I was so frustrated with Cyra's death, I almost became one of them, and that confused me even more. I didn't understand my thoughts. How could I blame Cyra for her own death?

"Maybe Chimmy spooked," Ben said, "and Cyra fell off and landed on the statue."

"Cyra never wore a helmet on trail rides," Martin said, shaking his head.

"Bonnie makes everyone wear a helmet in lessons and at shows," Ben said.

"But Cyra didn't wear one any other time," Martin added.

I didn't say anything. It was hard to believe that Cyra had died from falling off Chimmy. Cyra was an athlete, and Chimmy wasn't a spooky horse. Even if Chimmy had spooked, Cyra would have been able to stay on her back.

It didn't make sense. Maybe Chimmy had bucked or reared? No. I knew Chimmy and had never seen her buck or rear. Even if something had happened and Cyra had somehow lost her balance and fell, she would have pushed herself away from the statue and would not have allowed herself to crash into it. And there were no trees where she fell. And no rocks. The river rocks were all in a ring six feet away.

I couldn't make sense of what had happened. I asked Layne if she saw Cyra ride out bareback that morning and Layne nodded, tight-lipped.

"And with no helmet?"

Layne nodded again.

"Why did we let her?" I asked, remembering my rides with Cyra and that Cyra never wore a helmet.

"She is..." Layne dropped her head and sighed. "She was an adult. We couldn't make her wear a helmet if she didn't want to."

I wanted to scream, "Why didn't we TRY?" but didn't. It wouldn't be fair to take my frustration out on Layne.

How could Cyra be gone? She had been so happy, so full of hopes and dreams and courage and intelligence. It didn't make sense. And she had just gotten to know her sister. It wasn't fair. How could such a thing happen?

In the following days, a quiet sadness settled over the barn. Even the horses were quieter. Bonnie taught her lessons and refused to talk about what had happened. When the lessons were finished, she left the arena.

Layne taught lessons with long stretches of silence between instructions. She rode the young horses without joy, and left the barn early, not staying for evening chores or to do the little extras she had done in the past.

I stayed later than usual at the barn. I groomed Chimmy and helped Bonnie and Susan with evening chores and closing the barn. I didn't need to go home early, anyway. Al was in Pennsylvania again, working on another case.

When all the chores were finished, I went home for the night. Each evening, as I drove through Richmond and glanced in the direction of my mother's apartment above the garage, I felt a yearning to see her, but didn't want to upset her with the news. What could I tell her, anyway?

On the third evening following Cyra's death, I stopped at Chimmy's stall on my way out the door. I took Chimmy's handmade bridle off the hook on her stall door. No one had put it away in the tackroom since I hung it on her door the day Cyra died. I ran my fingers down the cheek piece and brought the rein to my nose, hoping I could smell Cyra on it, but it just smelled like leather. I sighed and hung the bridle back on the hook. Then I went into Chimmy's stall and buried my face in her neck.

The tears finally came. They slid out of my eyes. They were just there. Flowing. I sighed and the tears continued until I felt drained and exhausted. Chimmy stood quietly until I moved away from her. Then she put her nose against my chest.

"Thanks," I whispered. "I know you miss her, too."

13 - THE INVESTIGATION

In Michigan, cases of death due to unexplained or suspicious circumstances require an autopsy. Cyra's death was unexplained, so an autopsy was performed. But the autopsy determined only that the cause of death was "an impact with a blunt object." It could not confirm or deny that a fall from a horse caused Cyra's death. However, it did reveal that the marks on Cyra's skull did not correspond to any part of the statue.

When it was also confirmed that no trace of Cyra's hair or blood was found on the statue, two detectives were assigned to investigate further. A detective named John Monroe was placed in charge of the investigation, and a detective named Roland Phillips assisted him.

Detective Monroe called Centerline Farm while I was sitting in the office with Susan, waiting to write a check for my board and lessons with Bonnie or Layne. I wasn't sure, at that point, who I would be training with and each trainer charged different rates.

Susan answered the call, "Centerline Farm, Susan speaking."

I didn't mean to eavesdrop, but Detective Monroe had a loud voice, and it must have hurt Susan's ear because she held the phone away from her head. I could hear him clearly.

"Hello. This is Detective Monroe. I have been placed in charge of the investigation into the death of Cyra Black."

"How can I help you, Detective Monroe?" Susan's right hand tightened on her phone. Her left hand spread itself over the ledger she had just opened on her desk. Her body was rigid.

"I appreciate your cooperation, Ms?..."

"Please, just call me Susan."

"Susan. Okay. Thank you. I need a list of all people who were at the barn on the day of Ms. Black's death, and I need you to ask everyone on the list to meet us at the farm tomorrow at 1 pm to help us with the investigation. If they don't come voluntarily, we may have to issue a summons and they will be interviewed at the police station," he said.

Susan took a deep breath and relaxed her hands. "I will call them. I'm sure they will all be here. Everyone wants to know what happened."

"And you will provide me with a copy of the list?"

"Yes. Do you want it now or tomorrow?"

"Tomorrow will be fine. Thank you." I heard phone click, and the call was disconnected. Susan looked at it. "Well. Goodbye?" She looked at me and I shrugged.

I was standing outside Real's stall when the two detectives entered the barn on the following day. The first detective, tall and over-weight, I assumed was the loud Detective Monroe. The second detective, also tall, but thin, stood behind Detective Monroe. The two detectives stopped a few feet inside the entrance and looked up and down the barn aisle.

I thought they had probably never been in a stable before. "Are you looking for Susan?" I asked them.

Detective Monroe leaned forward. "Yes."

"She's in her office." I pointed down the aisle. "Do you want me to take you there?"

"No, thank you. We just wanted to look around before going to the office," he replied, and the two men walked down the aisle to Susan's office. I followed them down the aisle, just in case they needed help.

Susan must have heard them coming because she opened the office door, just as they approached it.

"Susan?" Detective Monroe asked.

Susan nodded. "You must be Detective Monroe?"

"Yes, and this is Detective Phillips. He is helping me with the investigation."

"Hello," Susan said. "I wish we were meeting under better circumstances."

"Yes. I agree. Susan, would you allow us to use your office to question the people who were here on the day of Ms Black's death?"

"Of course, Detective." Susan put her hand on the office door. "I'll gather my things and leave you to your work."

Officer Monroe cleared his throat. "I would like to question you first," he said.

Susan's mouth opened in surprise.

"You were here that day, am I correct?"

"Well, yes, I was."

"Then please stay. We would also like to talk to your daughter."

"Bonnie."

"Thank you. Bonnie. I understand she is one of the trainer's here and also part owner of Centerline Farm?"

Susan nodded, and I realized that Officer Monroe knew more than he was telling her. Susan opened the door to her office and she and the detectives walked inside. Detective Phillips closed the door behind them.

I decided to wait in the aisle, even though I didn't think I would be interviewed since I arrived at the barn after everyone else that day. I was joined in a few minutes by Layne, who leaned up against the wall and stared at the floor. Soon, Ben and Martin, Connie, Irene, Bonnie, and the working students joined us.

"They're questioning you too?" Connie asked Bonnie.

"Well, I was here so they want to talk to me too. Maybe it will help them put the pieces together."

After Susan was questioned, she opened her office door and nodded to Bonnie. I noticed that Susan's face was chalky-white.

After Bonnie was questioned, she opened the door and nodded to Layne. Bonnie's face also appeared to be drained of blood.

Layne moaned and entered the office. After about

fifteen minutes, she jerked open the door and pointed at me. Her face was red. "They want to see you next," she said.

I was surprised at being called but thought maybe I could help by telling them what I knew.

Detective Monroe was standing behind Susan's desk, talking to the other detective, when I entered the office. His size made Susan's desk look small, and he took up most of the space behind it. Detective Phillips was standing in the corner on his right.

Detective Monroe turned around as I entered the office. "Please sit down," he said, indicating the chair in front of Susan's desk.

Susan's chair squeaked in protest when Detective Monroe sat down after I was seated. He leaned forward, and the chair squeaked again.

"Marsha, may I call you by your first name?"

I nodded.

"I am, as you know, Detective John Monroe. This is my assistant, Detective Roland Phillips," he said nodding toward the man on his right. "You can just call each of us Detective, if that is easier for you."

"Alright," I said.

"I would like to ask you a few questions to help with our investigation. Detective Phillips will take notes. Is that okay with you?"

I nodded. "Sure."

"All right then. Marsha, where were you on the day of Cyra Black's death?"

I replied that I was at home and left Grosse Pointe around ten to come to the barn for a lesson with Bonnie. I watched Detective Phillips write down my answer to Detective Monroe's question.

"Should I have a lawyer with me?"

"You can," Detective Monroe said, sitting back in Susan's complaining chair. He knitted his hands together over his stomach. "It's your right. But we are just asking a few questions, trying to get a better understanding of what happened."

"Everyone wants to know what happened."

"I understand. So shall we proceed?" Detective Monroe moved forward and sat upright. The chair emitted a long squeak. He put his hands on the desk and folded them. "We just want to ask you a few more questions and examine your shoes."

"My shoes!" I couldn't hide my surprise.

"Yes. Please show us the shoes you wore to the barn on that day."

I looked down at my shoes.

"Let me explain," Detective Monroe leaned toward me and lowered his voice slightly. "Shoe impressions were found that seem inconsistent with an accident on horseback. Also, there were no hoof markings near the statue."

"Well, we often dismount in the area, and tie our horses to a tree or just ground-tie them so we can walk around the statue. Cyra told me that she and Layne erected it. Cyra said she wanted it there as a shrine to her mother." I saw Detective Phillips write something down and realized that I was nervous and probably talking too much.

"I see," Detective Monroe put his hands flat on the desk. "Well, would you let us see the shoes you wore on that day, or do you want a lawyer with you first?"

"No, I don't have any problems with that, I guess." I pulled my left boot off and handed it to the detective.

Detective Monroe took the shoe, but did not look at it. "Are these the shoes you wore to the barn on the day of Cyra Black's death?"

"Yes. I always wear these when I come to the barn. They are paddock boots. I add chaps to them when I ride."

"I see. May I have the other one too?"

"Oh. Okay." I removed the right boot and handed it to the detective.

Detective Monroe passed the boots to Detective Phillips, who looked at the bottoms of my boots and then at a photo he held next to them. He handed the boots back to Detective Monroe, who passed them back to me. I put my boots back on and wondered what they had just told him.

I was zipping up the second boot when Detective Monroe said, "I have one more question, Marsha. Did you have, or do you know of anyone who might have had, a problem with Cyra?"

I stopped breathing and sat up. "Is this a murder investigation?"

"Please, just answer the question."

I felt my face grow red.

Detective Monroe continued, "Layne told us earlier that your husband was seeing Cyra. Maybe you had a problem with her?"

I couldn't breathe. I felt as if someone had punched me in the stomach. I stood up. I was angry and took a deep breath. "I will be getting a lawyer. If you want to ask any more questions, you will have to do it in the presence of my lawyer."

"Very well. If we need to talk to you again, you will get a summons."

I stood up, feeling suddenly calm. I walked to the office door and turned around. "Detective Monroe, when you question Irene, she's... she was, I mean, she is, Cyra's sister."

Detective Monroe raised his eyebrows slightly. "Yes. Layne told us that they were estranged."

I hesitated, wanting to say more, but decided against it. Maybe I had already said too much.

"I would like to talk to Irene next, if you don't mind letting her know?"

I left the office door open and nodded to Irene. She understood and entered the office, head down. I stayed in the hallway to see what would happen next.

Layne was standing by the door to the parking lot, leaning against the door, her back to the others. I walked over to Layne and stood there.

Layne slowly turned her head in my direction. "Did

he tell you to stick around too?"

I found myself nodding yes, even though Detective Monroe had not asked me to stay.

Layne sighed. "Good. It's not just me, then."

Detective Monroe and Detective Phillips emerged from Susan's office. Irene was with them. They walked over to Layne and me.

Detective Phillips spoke, "Layne Madison, you are under arrest for 'reasonable suspicion' concerning the death of Cyra Black." He began to read Layne her rights from a sheet of paper he pulled from his shirt pocket as Detective Monroe handcuffed her.

Layne's face grew red, and she moaned, "Noooo..." and shook her head slowly.

I turned to Irene and was shocked to discover that Irene was also in handcuffs. Her face was white, and she was staring at Layne. She turned her head to me. "I did not kill my sister," she whispered hoarsely.

I was frozen and speechless. I watched the detectives walk Layne and Irene to the parking lot and put them in their car. As they drove away, I pulled out my cell phone and called Joey. I let him know that Irene and Layne had been arrested and were on the way to the police station.

Joey was not emotional. He listened and thanked me.

Then I called Al. To my surprise, he answered his cell phone right away. I told him about the questioning and Irene's and Layne's arrest.

"What?" He shouted into the phone. "You answered questions without me?"

I flinched. I should have called Al first, of course, but he was out of town again, and he never called me back right away. "I only answered a few," I said.

"I don't care! Never talk to a detective without a lawyer present! You, of all people, should know that!" After a pause, during which I could almost hear Al calming himself down, he asked, "Who else was questioned?"

"Susan and Bonnie."

"And I suppose no one had their lawyer present?"

"No one had a lawyer."

I could feel the heat of Al's anger over the phone. "Marsha," he said slowly, "you know better than anyone that anything you say can be used against you in court, but a detective cannot hold your silence against you as evidence of guilt. You also know that it's a legally accepted and very effective interrogation technique to lie to you and present false evidence in an effort to obtain information. Do not talk to anyone else without me. Do you understand?"

I was getting angry. "Yes, Al, I understand. But I did nothing wrong. I'm not afraid."

"That doesn't matter. You could be totally innocent, but incriminate yourself anyway. Don't talk to anyone else without me, please?" Al had softened his voice. "I love you," he added.

I sighed. "I love you too. I wish you were here. Come home soon." I said goodbye before Al realized I was crying.

Al flew home from Pennsylvania that afternoon. He drove directly home from the airport and found me sitting on the patio, holding a cup of coffee. I had changed out of my barn clothes but never made it into the shower. Instead, I poured myself a cup of coffee and sat on the patio, just holding it.

I didn't hear Al drive into the garage or walk through the house, and I was startled when he opened the patio door. I jumped up, dropping the cup, which shattered, splashing coffee on my legs and my fluffy white bathrobe.

Al scooped me into his arms and held me. When he released me, we went into the kitchen where I poured coffee for both of us, placed them on the breakfast nook table and sat down facing Al.

"Tell me about the interviews," he said gently.

"There were two detectives," I said, curling my hands around the coffee cup. "Detective Monroe was in charge, and Detective Phillips took notes. They questioned us in the office at the barn. They asked all the boarders who were there that day to be present, but they only questioned five of us: Susan, Bonnie, Layne, Irene and me. I guess they found what they were looking for."

Al nodded and asked what questions they had

asked me. I told him about the questions and the examination of my shoes. I told him I had stopped the interview after that, and Al relaxed a little.

"But Layne and Irene were arrested," I said.

"Why Layne and Irene?"

"I think it had something to do with their shoes. The detectives looked at the soles of my shoes. They probably asked Layne and Irene the same questions they asked me, and they probably looked at their shoes, too. Layne and Irene usually wear the same style barn shoes."

Al groaned. "They're in custody now?"

"Well, they might be, but maybe not. I called Joey, and he probably bailed them out."

"Okay. I'll check with Joey."

Al pulled out his cell phone and called Joey. He learned that Joey had posted bond for both women.

Al said, "Joey met them at the police station with the bondsman. They were released and Joey dropped Layne off at her house."

I sighed, and Al reached over the table and rubbed my shoulder. Then he stood up and pulled me up and into his arms. I buried my face in his chest and he kissed my head. "You smell like a horse," he said. "I'm starting to like it."

14 - THE ARREST

Susan was irritated. She was sitting at her desk, talking to me, or maybe at me. I think she just needed to vent. "Layne has been gone for two days. I tried to reach her by phone, but she didn't answer. I left messages. Nothing. Then she walked in this morning without a word to me and started teaching!"

There was a knock on the door.

I was grateful for the interruption. "I'll get it. I need to check on Real, anyway." Real was fine, but I really needed to escape. I didn't know what to say to Susan, and I didn't want to comment on whatever was going on with Layne, so I was grateful for the interruption.

Detective Monroe opened the door before I could get out of my chair. Detective Phillips was standing behind him.

Susan and I stood up. "Hello, Detectives. What can I do for you?" Susan said.

"Good morning, Mrs. Heins. Good morning, Mrs. Myers." The detectives nodded at us, and I wondered why they were being so formal, when they had used our first names during the interviews. "We are looking for Layne Madison."

"She's in the indoor arena, giving a lesson." Susan consulted her watch. "She should be finished in a few minutes. Would you like a coffee?"

"No thanks," Detective Monroe answered for both of them. "Will you show us where the indoor arena is?"

"Certainly," Susan frowned, pocketed her cell phone and stood. "Please follow me."

I didn't check on Real. I followed Susan and the detectives and thought, now what?

I stood at the rail with Susan and the detectives, and watched as Meghan, one of the working students, took a lesson on Prakseda. I tried to concentrate on the lesson, but all I was aware of was the smell of the detectives' uniforms, and their aftershave or cologne. I could also smell the underlying oily smell most men have, no matter how much cologne they use. I felt like I was too close to something dangerous, but I couldn't leave.

"Layne" Susan said when Layne turned from her student to look at us, "you remember Detective Monroe and Detective Phillips? They are here to talk to you."

"Yes, I remember," Layne said and turned back to her student. "That will be all for today," she said to Meghan, and walked over to the rail.

Detective Monroe said, "Are you Layne Madison?"

Layne frowned and said, "Yes, you know who I am!"

Detective Monroe said, "Layne Madison, I am placing you under arrest for the murder of Cyra Black. Detective Phillips, please read Mrs. Madison her rights."

I didn't look at Susan, but I almost felt her catch her breath and stiffen. Or maybe I just imagined it, because that's exactly what I did.

Detective Phillips began reading from a card he produced from his shirt pocket. "Layne Madison, you have the right to remain silent. Anything you say can be used against you. You have the right to have an attorney present before and during questioning. If you cannot afford the services of an attorney, you have the right to have one appointed, at public expense and without cost to you, to represent you before and during questioning. Do you understand your rights?"

Layne looked at me, then at the detective. "Yes," she said crisply, and then she looked at Susan and said, "You never liked me."

Susan's mouth quivered, but she clamped her lips shut and turned away from Layne.

Detective Phillips brought out his handcuffs and asked Layne to turn around. The he placed the handcuffs on her wrists and put his hand on Layne's elbow. "Please come this way," he said.

Layne snatched her elbow away from his hand and marched ahead of the detectives, who walked behind her to the barn entrance and into the parking lot.

Susan and I followed them to the barn door.

When they reached the police car, Detective Phillips opened the back door for Layne, and she stepped inside the vehicle. Detective Phillips fastened her seat belt and closed the back door, then got into the passenger seat. Detective Monroe got into the driver's seat and started the car's engine. When the police car moved past Susan and I before exiting the parking lot, Layne was looking away from us.

Susan was the first to speak. "When Bonnie hired her, I thought it was a mistake. Layne is right. I never liked her."

"Did you know something about her?" I asked.

"No, Bonnie hired her over the phone. When I met her, I didn't like her. But Bonnie liked her credentials. It's true that she is talented and hard working. She does a great job for us. Or did. This is awful," Susan said, shaking her head.

I said nothing, but I thought about my first visit to Centerline and how Susan had accepted me without question. I watched Susan walk back toward the office and sighed. Then I thought about my own uneasiness in Layne's presence.

Over a late dinner that night, I asked Al to go talk to Layne and, possibly, represent her.

"I can't," he said.

"We need to help her. If she killed Cyra, she didn't do it on purpose. I'm sure of that."

"I can talk to her, but only as a friend. I can't be her lawyer."

"Why not? I know she doesn't have a lot of money, but..."

"It's not the money," Al interrupted. "I'm too close

to the case to feel comfortable taking it. You were her friend and Cyra's, too."

I thought about it and sighed. Al was right. I could understand the conflict. I felt bad for Layne, but I would probably hate her if I knew she willfully killed Cyra.

Al reached over the table and raised my chin. I had to look at him. "Are you mad at me for that?"

"No. I understand. And I don't think Layne was ever anyone's friend. I think she was too ambitious to be a friend. She used everyone to get what she wanted."

Al said nothing. He just wiped a tear off my cheek.

15 - SAYING GOODBYE

I was brushing Real when Irene walked into the barn. I watched her slowly walk toward me and thought, even her walk has changed.

I put my brush down and put Real in his stall. Irene watched and waited. I couldn't think of anything to say, so I hugged her. She hugged me back, and I held on to her for a long time. Maybe it was too long, but she didn't move away. Finally, I released her.

Irene sighed. "Thanks."

I wanted to say something, but I couldn't think of anything, so I just looked at her hands.

Irene was holding a stack of envelopes, and she handed one to me. "It's the burial place, the time, and a note about the funeral service."

"Al and I will be there."

Irene nodded. "Thank you. I want to hand these out in person, but not everyone will be at the barn today. Will you and Bonnie hand them out to the people I miss?"

"Of course," I said. "Where will you leave them?"

"In Bonnie's office."

"Okay. We will take care of it."

I gave Irene another hug and she hugged me back. She released me and let her hand slide down my arm.

When her hand reached mine, she held it for a moment, gave it a little squeeze, and released it. Then she turned and walked away.

I watched her walk slowly down the barn aisle and thought she was being very strong, like her name, Ituha.

When she turned the corner in the aisle, I opened the envelope. Inside was a printed card with funeral information and a hand-written note from Irene. The note said:

Dear friend,

Cyra/Enola will be buried in Clinton Township, not Pyramid Lake. I want her here, with me and her friends, where she had happy times. Although our mother is buried in Pyramid Lake, I cannot send her back there, where our misery began.

We will observe some of our tribal customs during the funeral service. Personal items are often placed in the coffin. Enola's coffin would be open if you want to leave something with her.

I will speak at the service, and if you wish to speak, please do. I also ask that you dress in colors as well as black clothing to symbolize our belief that death is a doorway to another life.

The location and time of the funeral service is on a card included with this note. I hope you will be there.

Irene/Ituha

The day of the funeral was warm with a gentle

breeze. Sunlight filtered through the oak trees, sending sparkles of light along the path as Al and I walked to the spot chosen for Cyra's body. Cyra's friends from the barn were there, along with Jay and her co-workers from the club.

We gathered around the coffin and Irene said, "Enola's body has been washed and wrapped in a shroud, according to Indian tradition. Also, according to tradition, the coffin is a simple wooden box, and no embalming is allowed." Irene dropped her head and paused a minute.

Everyone waited. Some dropped their heads.

Then Irene spoke again. "I asked everyone to wear colors as well as black to symbolize the Indian belief that death is not the end, but the beginning of another life. I've put branches from an evergreen tree around the coffin for the same reason."

Then Irene walked a step closer to the coffin and spoke to her sister's body, "Enola, my sister, you never abandoned me, although I betrayed your love. It was your love that saved me from eternal agony. You never knew hate because you never forgot, as I did, that there are always three reasons for everything that is."

Irene raised her head and spoke. I could see that her eyes were filled with tears, but her voice was strong. "Indians know that each living creature must find its proper place in the world. Enola found hers when she came here. I found mine when she reminded me of who I am. Enola has touched every one of you.

She lives in all of us as she continues her journey. She will always be with us."

Irene walked to the coffin and lifted her hand. "My tears go with your body, my sweet Enola," and she wiped her eyes with a handkerchief and placed it in the coffin, then moved away.

There was a moment of awkwardness, and Al nudged me. I stepped up to the coffin. "Cyra, my friend, I miss you. I will always hunger for the days that were taken from us. I treasure the days we had. You will always be in my thoughts."

I took a deep breath and continued, "A piece of the pottery we made together goes with your body, but your love stays in my heart." I lowered a small white dish into the coffin with a sob and stepped back to Al, who put his arm around me.

Bonnie and Susan came forward next. Susan spoke as Bonnie placed two small cotton bags in the coffin. "This is sand from Centerline Farm and a braid of hair from Chimmy's mane. We love you, Cyra-Enola. We will never forget the lessons you taught us."

Ben and Martin stepped forward, and each put a small stone into the coffin. "From the stream behind the farm," Ben said. "River rocks we found on our rides together," Martin completed.

And so it went, each person stepping forward to say goodbye and leave a small token in the coffin with Cyra.

After the coffin was closed, Irene poured a vial of

water over it. "Water from Pyramid Lake," she said.

The coffin was slowly lowered into the grave. Irene put a shovel full of earth on it and everyone watched as caretakers completed the burial, shovel by shovel.

When all the earth had been returned to the grave and shaped into a small mound, Irene laid a blanket of flowers on it.

We stood in silence for a moment, then left.

16 - THE VISIT

Layne was awaiting trial in the county jail. I walked in the door and was immediately depressed by the brown wood and glass reception desk and off-white walls. There was nothing comforting in sight, and I wanted to turn around and leave, but I had come to see Layne so I swallowed my feelings.

I walked up to the glass enclosed desk, my hesitant steps echoing on the tile floor.

"May I help you?" a uniformed woman asked, unsmiling.

"I came to visit an inmate."

"I will need to see your ID."

I opened my wallet and gave her my driver's license.

The uniformed woman wrote my name and license number in a log book and handed the license back to me. "And who are you here to visit?"

"Layne Madison."

She wrote Layne's name down, consulted her watch, and wrote the time of day in her log book. "Please wait for an escort. You can wait over there." She pointed to a corner of the room with four chairs.

"And I have some money for her." I brought money for Layne, but Al told me that I couldn't give it to her directly. It would have to be deposited in her account at the jail. I decided to bring money after learning that inmates were fed three times a day and were given jail clothing, two blankets, two sheets, and a bar of soap. That was it. If they wanted anything else, they had to depend upon money sent to them by family and friends. So I brought money.

"I can take that for you," the uniformed woman said.

I opened my wallet and pulled out the money I brought for Layne and pushed it through the glass at the woman.

She took the money, counted it and said, "Three hundred dollars."

"Yes."

She wrote in the ledger by the other information she had entered and opened a second book that was on the counter by her right hand. She put the money in a drawer below her desk, then wrote in her second book and tore a page from it. She handed the page to me.

It was a receipt. "Deposited $300.00 to account of inmate number 955006, Layne Madison," and the date.

"Please have a seat and wait for an escort," she said.

Instead of going to the corner chairs, as I was told, I wandered over to the kiosk in the corner of the lobby and purchased what was labeled as a "care package." It contained a toothbrush, toothpaste and a hair brush. I also purchased a bag of chocolates and a science fiction novel. I held the care package and gifts in front of me like a shield as I waited for the guard to escort me to a common room where I would be allowed to see Layne.

Al had told me I would probably be allowed to visit Layne, supervised at a distance by guards in a room where other inmates were also receiving visitors.

The guard arrived 10 minutes later. "You are here to see Layne Madison," he said. It might have been a question, but it sounded as if he were stating a fact, so I just nodded.

"Follow me," he said and led me to a metal detector.

"Your cell phone and your purse, please."

I gave them to him, and he put them in a plastic tray. He took the plastic tray to a wall that looked like a post office wall of mailboxes, opened a box, put the tray inside and closed the box. Then he gave me a key fob. It had a number on it.

Then he examined the care package and flipped through the pages of the novel. He removed the wrapper on the box of chocolates and looked inside the box. Satisfied, he returned the package, the chocolates and the novel to me.

"Please walk through the metal detector," he said.

I walked through the metal detector.

"Please follow me."

He led me to a room with white walls, greyish floors and plastic tables and chairs. I was told to sit at a table and wait. I sat and looked around the room. There were several tables occupied by inmates and their visitors. The inmates wore orange pants and orange tops that looked like hospital scrubs. I knew the purpose of the orange color was to make the inmates obvious in any area and allow them to be easily supervised by the guards. Three guards were standing at different places around the room. They did not attempt to talk to each other, but were constantly scanning the room, watching for any sign of trouble.

After a few minutes, Layne was brought in. She walked slowly to the table, escorted by her female guard. She pulled out a chair and sat down, placing her hands on the table. I noticed, then, that all the inmates in the room had their hands on the tables.

Layne's guard left her with me and retreated to stand by the wall.

"Hi Layne."

"Hi."

Layne's eyes were larger than I remembered. They had a glazed appearance.

"It's good to see you. I'm glad I came. You look good. I was afraid that you would be distraught."

"I've been there, and I got over it. This is the way it is. I've got to make life better now. I can't stay in the hole I fell in."

I nodded. I pushed the care package, novel and chocolate over to Layne. "Here."

"Thanks. They sent a message that you made a deposit in my account. Thank you for that. It really helps. My husband won't come here."

"Oh. I'm sorry to hear that. Everyone at the barn

said to say hello."

"I'll bet!" Layne scoffed. "They're probably glad I'm locked up!"

"No one's glad, Layne. But I think they're afraid to come see you. They don't know what your attitude is and they're afraid they don't really know you now."

Layne frowned.

"Don't you think that's normal?"

"Sure, I do. I feel the same way. I don't know who I am, and I think my husband will divorce me. I'll be alone."

Layne was bouncing the heel of her right foot off the floor and her hands had balled up into fists. The guard who had brought her to the table left the wall and started walking toward us. Layne put her right hand up and then let it float down to the table. She stretched out the fingers of both hands flat on the table. I understood that she was physically telling the guard, "Okay, I'll calm down. I'll be okay."

Layne dropped her head and stared at the table as she talked. "I didn't mean to cause trouble. You know that? I never meant to. I didn't set out to do anything but talk to Cyra and get it off my chest." Her voice faded.

I nodded. I wanted to comfort Layne, but I had been told not to touch a prisoner. "Do you want to tell me about it? Would that make you feel better?"

"I don't know if it's possible to feel better now." Layne said.

"Tell me what happened. It might make you feel better."

Layne looked up. Her eyes didn't meet mine but looked over my shoulder, staring into the distance as she started talking.

"We were the only ones at the barn that morning. It was early. 6 am. I was surprised to see Cyra come in that early, but she said she couldn't sleep, so she came to ride. She helped me grain and hay the horses. We filled the water buckets inside and the troughs outside. Then we turned the horses out.

"Cyra kept Chimmy in so she could ride. She groomed her, then she put that bridle on her. The one she made. I asked her if she was riding inside or out, and she said she wanted to go on a trail ride. I said I would go with her, so I grabbed a horse and saddled up."

"Which horse?"

Layne either didn't hear me, or she ignored my question. "We went out on the trail. It was a beautiful day. Not too hot. A nice breeze. Clear blue sky. The air smelled clean, and it was easy to breathe. Not like here." Layne's eyes darted to the left of the room. "Sometimes all you smell here is urine, disinfectant, and body odor. You never realize how much it means to be able to walk outside and look at the sky whenever you want to until you're locked up." Layne stopped speaking.

I didn't know what to say.

After a few moments, Layne started talking again. "It was a beautiful day. The birds were making their happy noises. The purple martins were flying around, grabbing insects out of the air. And there weren't any flies to annoy the horses. It was a perfect day.

"We went down the trail and looked at the trees and the new growth around them. Cyra pointed out the new wildflowers. She always watched for the new growth. She could predict what kind of fall weather we would have by the spring and summer growth. In the fall, she knew what kind of winter we would have."

I nodded, hoping Layne would continue. She still wasn't looking at me. Instead, her eyes were focused somewhere on the wall behind my head.

She started talking again. "We rode, and I wanted to tell her that I was really happy that she and Irene had found each other, but every time I thought about it, I got angry because, if they hadn't, I would still be the trainer, running my own farm with Irene. But now that Cyra was in the picture, Irene changed. She didn't care about building a business anymore. She lost her ambition. She old me the day before that she didn't want to buy a farm. She said all she wanted to do was spend more time with Cyra. She even forgot my birthday!" Layne drummed the fingers of her right hand as she talked, clearly getting upset again.

The guard took notice, and once again, moved in our direction. Layne stopped drumming her fingers and spread them out on the table, then relaxed them into a cupped position. The guard returned to her position on the wall.

"We came to the stream." Layne lowered her eyes, as if looking at the stream.

"It was clear, and I could see tadpoles darting about. And the stones that Cyra loved so much were wet and glistening. We stopped and picked up a couple. Then we got back on our horses and crossed the stream."

Layne paused, then smiled. "On the other side, across the meadow, we saw a doe. The doe saw us, but didn't run off, just raised her head up and sniffed. We were able to get really close before she turned and walked into the woods." Layne starred at the wall above my head.

"We rode into the woods and then up the path to the statue. Then we got off the horses and added the stones to the ring around the statue, like we always did." Layne made a gesture with her right hand, and I realized she was putting a stone in the ring around the statue in her mind.

"Cyra picked up a yellowish stone we had found on our last trail ride. It was large and had rings of a darker brown running through it. She turned it over in her hands and she said it looked like there was a fossil embedded in it."

Layne opened her hand, palm up. "I asked to see it and she handed me the stone. It weighed about four pounds. I turned the stone over and looked. I could see that it had something in it, but I didn't know if it was a fossil or not." Layne looked at her hand.

"Cyra went closer to the statue and squtted down in front of it. She would always do that and stare at the statue for a while. She said, "Irene told me she doesn't want to buy a farm. She wants to stay at Centerline."

"I was standing there. and I got a big knot in my stomach. It would have been better if she hadn't said anything at all. Then maybe I would have had time to get over it. To get over the years of hard work and waiting for my luck to change!" Layne's hand closed into a fist.

I was suddenly angry. Cyra was dead, and all Layne was thinking about was herself? I shouldn't have said it, but I did. "And maybe Cyra wouldn't be dead?"

Layne didn't see the change in me. "Yeah. She said she was really sorry that it didn't work out and I told her I was sorry too. Really, really sorry." Layne's hands had balled into fists, lying flat on the table. The guard was watching and straightened up a little.

Layne rubbed her right fist on the table. "She just kept talking and talking, saying how she thought it was probably best, anyway, since Irene didn't need to work that hard and worry about making a business succeed. I told her it would have been my work to make it succeed, not Irene's!" Layne's fists tightened and I could see that the knuckles were white where the blood had left them.

"She said that I needed to finish Grand Prix, get my gold medal and then get a sponsor so I could go to

Europe." Layne's right fist rotated on the table.

"I told her that I didn't need her to tell me what to do, and she shouldn't tell Irene what to do!"

Layne took a deep breath and spoke in a low growl, "Irene was my sponsor until SHE took her away from me. I worked hard all my life for a chance to get my own farm, to be a trainer and to run my own life. It was MY goal! It was what I wanted." The volume of Layne's voice began to rise, "I had coddled Irene when she was a bitch to everyone and rode her horses and kissed her ass for the chance to make MY dreams come true and then SHE came along and changed EVERYTHING!" Layne's fist pounded the table.

The guard was at the table in seconds and covered Layne's fist with her hand. Layne snatched it away, jumped off her chair and hit the guard. The guard grabbed Layne's arm, spun her around and tried to restrain her. Layne pulled away from her, screaming, "Let me go! Let - me - GO!"

Suddenly a second guard was at the table. The two guards grabbed Layne and pulled her arms behind her back. Then they put her in handcuffs and tried to pull her away from the table, but Layne pulled back toward me, her neck stretched out, her eyes bulging. "Yes! I killed her! She destroyed everything I had worked for all my life! I smashed her with the rock! I SMASHED HER AND SMASHED HER AND SMASHED HER!" Layne struggled as the guards pulled her away. Her cheeks were wet. She was crying.

I sat in the chair and watched until the doors closed behind Layne and the guards. Then I took a deep breath, stood and pushed myself away from the table. My hands were shaking.

EPILOGUE

Layne Madison was eventually tried and convicted of voluntary manslaughter. She received a sentence of 15 years in prison and a fine of $7,500, the maximum allowed by Michigan law.

Layne's husband divorced her and left the state.

While incarcerated, Layne received counseling for anger management. She attended college online and earned an associate's degree. She convinced the parole board that she was a changed person, ready to take her place in society as a responsible adult capable of patience, forgiveness and understanding. She served only five years of her 15 year sentence.

It was an act worthy of an Oscar. Layne had some scores to settle, and she kept a numbered list in her head.

...continued in **EXTENDED TROT** *on page 185*

EXTENDED TROT
Irene's story

DEDICATION

For my mother who taught me how to be strong.

17 - CHIMMY

Two days after her sister's funeral, Irene walked back into the barn. I was grooming Real and watched her walk slowly down the aisle. She was holding Cyra's handmade bridle.

I stopped brushing Real and looked at the bridle. Then I looked at Irene.

"I want to keep this," Irene said, stroking the length of the bridle, "but I want you to have Chimmy."

My heart twisted in my chest. "Irene, are you sure?"

"I want you to have her," she repeated. "I could keep her, but I wouldn't ride her. She's too small for my long legs, and I couldn't ride her even if my legs were short. I would be crying all the time."

It was true. Irene was a retired model, and she had the longest legs I had ever seen. Even though she was beautiful and graceful, Irene would look silly if she tried to ride Chimmy, a small horse, more suited to a short rider, like me. And I would look ridiculous if I rode the horses Irene owned.

Cyra had been my best friend, even when Irene hated her, and I was touched that Irene wanted to give me the little blue roan mare instead of selling her.

"Thanks, Irene. I'll take good care of her."

"I know you will, and you're welcome."

I hesitated, then said, "Irene, When I was with Cyra, she opened a checking and savings account. You're the beneficiary listed on the accounts. It's the money she was saving to go to Florida."

Irene turned her head away and looked down the barn aisle. She was probably remembering what a fit she threw when she learned that Cyra was planning to go to Florida for the winter and train with Bonnie, her and a few other Centerline Farm clients. Finally, Irene turned back to me and said, "I don't want it."

"She would want you to have it."

Irene shook her head. "No. I can't take it. Will you take it? Go to Florida with us?"

"I can't. Susan asked me to help manage the farm while you and the others go to Florida. I said I would."

Irene managed a little smile. "That's great," she said. "But I thought they would just hire another trainer."

"They're looking for one, but Susan wants to take her time and choose carefully. She told Bonnie it was her turn to choose a trainer."

Irene smiled a little more. "Well, sit this winter out, but go with us next year, okay?"

"I will, and I'll take both horses. I think I'll be ready by then."

Irene nodded. "You'll be ready. Okay. We will leave the money in the account and use it for Chimmy's expenses in Florida next year. That would make Cyra happy."

I nodded and looked at Irene's serene, but sad, face.

"Do you feel like lunch? We haven't had a chance to talk since the funeral."

"Sure," Irene said. "That would be nice."

"Okay. Do you want to go to the restaurant where my mother works? I'd like you to meet her."

Irene smiled. "That would be nice. I want to meet the woman who raised you."

It was the end of the lunch rush when we arrived at the restaurant. We chose an abandoned table at the back and pushed the left over dishes down to the end of the table. A few minutes later, a busboy cleared the dishes and wiped the table with a damp cloth.

"Marsha! What a nice surprise." My mother bent down and hugged my shoulders with her left arm.

"Mom, this is Irene, Cyra's sister. I told you about Cyra, but you never met her."

My mother reached out and touched Irene's shoulder. "I'm sorry to hear about your sister."

"Thank you," Irene replied.

"I'm very happy to finally meet you. Marsha talks about you all the time."

"And Marsha tells me you're the best mother ever."

"I don't know about that, but alright, I'll take the compliment, and I'll take your orders. You must be starving."

After lunch, we lingered over our coffee, but I could see that Irene was getting restless. Maybe she had an appointment. Or maybe she was just bored. Irene was always in motion, shopping, riding, or driving her Maserati.

"What's wrong, Irene? Do you want to leave?"

Irene shook her head and rapped her knuckles on the table. "I need to ask you something," she said.

"Okay."

Irene spread her hands and stroked the table. "Why was Cyra the one so many people abused? Why does one person have to suffer so much? I should have been the one Layne killed. It should have been me."

I could see tears starting to form in Irene's eyes. "Irene," I said slowly, "I know you've been hurt, too. I can see it. It wasn't just Cyra."

Irene sighed, but said nothing.

I lightly touched Irene's hand with my finger, then rested my hand by hers. "Maybe you should tell me your story. Maybe you would feel better if you told me what happened between you and Cyra. Your story is safe with me."

Irene nodded but said nothing.

After a minute, I said, "Why did you go away and leave your mother and Cyra? Why did you return eight years later and take Cyra away?" I stopped, afraid I had said too much.

After a long sigh, Irene said, finally, "I didn't."

"But Cyra said you left one day and never came back until you came for her."

Irene nodded, "That's true." She wrapped her

hands around her coffee cup. "I've tried to forget everything that happened, but it never leaves me."

"Would you feel better if you talked about it now, after so many years of not talking?"

"Maybe. Joey knows now, but no one else. Cyra and I told him everything after we had our time together. Cyra didn't know what had happened. She thought I had run away with the creep who drove me back home to get her. So I had to tell her first. Then, with her permission, I told Joey."

"That must have been hard on you."

"It was. I thought Joey would divorce me, but I had to tell him. He cried. I felt awful."

I remembered the times I had watched Joey with Irene. He adored Irene. Joey was a rich and powerful man. Irene was lucky. She was also lucky that Joey had never found out what a bitch she had been at the barn before her reunion with Cyra. But that was in the past. An amazing transformation had taken place in Irene when she realized that the almost 20-year-old Cyra was her sister, who she had last seen at ten years of age.

"Joey loves you, Irene. He will always love you. No matter what."

Irene nodded and stroked her coffee cup. "Yes," she said, her voice breaking. "But I didn't expect it."

Irene cleared her throat and began to tell her story:

Everyone at the farm thinks I am a retired model, but I never modeled.

It happened when I was 12 and Cyra, whose name was Enola, was 4 years old. We rode to work that day, the same as any other day. The best part of each day was going to work and coming home again because we rode our ponies there and back.

You know we are Indians. Paiute Indians. We lived near Pyramid Lake in Nevada. Half of us were unemployed, but our mother had a job. Our mother, who we called Gaho, worked at a motel, cleaning rooms. We worked with her.

Usually we just walked our ponies, but sometimes we could get Gaho to go a bit faster. I would ask her to race me, but Gaho wouldn't do it. So Enola and I - we rode together on my pony - would canter ahead and then circle back to her. Gaho didn't mind, as long as we didn't get out of sight.

When we got to work, we left our ponies in a pen behind the motel. We gave them some hay we brought with us and water from the motel. They were happy to eat and sleep in the sun while we worked. There was a little shade created by a tarp the owner of the motel put up for us, and they could sleep in the shade if the sun got too hot.

We worked cleaning rooms and doing laundry. It was a big motel, laid out in an "H" pattern, with the office and storerooms on one side and the vending machines and ice maker on the other side.

I was cleaning on one side of the motel and Gaho and Cyra were cleaning at the other side. Cyra was really too young to clean, but she tried to help Gaho. We always made a game of it. We cleaned and tried to see who could finish quicker.

I was pushing my cleaning cart down the outside when a man stepped out in front of my cart.

"I want some extra towels," he said and held a five dollar bill out to me. It was common to tip for extras, and that was a big tip, so I got the towels from the bottom of my cart and reached out for the five as I was giving him the towels. He caught both of my hands, twirled me around and put his hand over my mouth so fast that I didn't have time to scream.

Before I knew it, I was in the back seat of a car with him. Another man, who was sitting in the front seat, drove us away from the motel.

The man who grabbed me was holding me in the back seat had his hand over my mouth and I bit him.

"You little bitch! Do that again and you'll be sorry!"

The man in the front just looked at him in the rear view mirror and laughed.

I started screaming and the man in the back seat yelled at me again, "Shut up!"

I narrowed my eyes at him and screamed some more.

"Don't bother," the man who was driving said, looking back at me in the rear view mirror. "No one can hear you," and he turned on the car radio.

It was true. We were on a desert road. Occasionally, a car would pass us, going in the opposite direction, but they didn't even look at us. They took me to a woman's house. There were other girls and boys there. I was locked in a room by myself with a bucket to use as a toilet. They opened the door once a day and shoved a tray of food in. I threw it at the door. I bashed my fists against the walls for three days. When I knew it wouldn't do any good, I stopped hurting myself. I was miserable, hungry, dirty, and I had cried out all my tears.

After five days, the same man who grabbed me at the motel opened the door.

I screamed.

He just grabbed me and took me to a bathroom. "Wash yourself," he told me. "I'll wait outside," he said.

There were no windows in the bathroom. I sat on the floor and screamed. Then I kicked and pounded on the door. The man outside the door just laughed and said, "I'll be here for as long as it takes. When you are clean, if you are good, I will feed you and let you join the other kids."

After a while, I washed. It felt better to be clean. I put the clean clothes on that were in the bathroom and kicked the door.

When the door opened, I came out fighting, but he was ready for me. "Now let's see how good you are," he said and took me to another bedroom where he raped me.

It hurt, and I bled so much I thought I would die.

Afterwards, he tied me to the bed, leaving my right hand free. Then he brought me a plate of food, and I threw it at him.

He shrugged and said, "Your choice," and left.

I didn't see him again until he brought another girl to the house a year later. I was told that he was paid $1,000 for each girl and he got to "de-flower" each one as a bonus, if no customer had reserved a virgin.

The next day, the other kids came to see me. There were five of them, three girls and two boys. They said they were also locked in a room and raped, like I had been. They sat on the bed and told me their stories. They were all from poor families or single-parent families, like mine. All of them had been taken by force, like me. They had been locked in a room and raped. But now they weren't locked in their rooms and they were all walking around free.

I didn't understand. I asked them, "Why don't you leave?"

"Where would we go?" a young boy said. "We don't have any money. What would we do?"

"Run!" I said. "Go to the police! Tell them what happened!"

He just shook his head. "The police just find us and they bring us back. She adopted us," he said.

"We can't leave until we are 18," one of the girls told me.

Somehow, this woman, who was called Rusha, had legally adopted all the kids in the house. After the kids left, Rusha came into my room. I was still tied to the bed by my left hand. She looked at the bloody sheets and bent over to untie my left hand.

"In certain cultures, that would be worth a lot of money," she said, and pointed to the blood. "But in this country, it isn't valued."

I spat on her, and she slapped me.

"You will learn to be obedient," she said. "You will be obedient or you will suffer the consequences. Now be good!"

I spat on her again, but she didn't slap me again. She just opened the door and a man, a different man, came into the room and picked me up. He locked me in another room with only a bare mattress and a bucket. I wasn't tied up but I had to stay there for two weeks. Again, I got a bucket to use for a toilet and one meal a day.

I wanted to die. I wanted to kill myself. But there was nothing in that room to use: no sheets or curtains to use to hang myself and no sharp objects. I tried to suffocate myself, but my body rebelled. By the time they let me out, my spirit was almost broken.

That's when my pony came to save me. Every time I wanted to give up, he was there. Sometimes he was just there, standing by me. Sometimes I could only smell him, but sometimes I could feel him touch my cheek and feel his warm breath on my face.

At the end of two weeks, I was put in the bathroom again. I bathed. They took me out, and I was put in a clean bedroom. The kids came to see me again. They fed me and I ate. Then they told me I would be put in a mental hospital if I continued to fight. Or at least that's what Rusha told them would happen.

They called her Rusha. I learned later that Rusha means "a cruel person" and "a deliberate sinner." She was. And no one dared give her a nickname.

She had legal custody of each child, but none of them called her "Mom." A month after I went there, she showed me my adoption papers. My new name was Irene.

Every once in a while, sgmeone from the state's child protective services would come by to check on us, but they only checked to see if we were healthy and were being home-schooled.

The kids told me I could leave when I turned 18, but the oldest boy was nineteen. I think he was afraid to leave. He had never been out in the world since Rusha took him as a three-year-old. He was comfortable, and he had a few privileges, like Saturdays at the movies. I think he was also cruel, like Rusha. He seemed to be watching me and the other kids, and I didn't trust him.

I never accepted being there. I got into trouble all the time. I was never taken anywhere outside the house because I fought them and tried to run. I broke things, and I tore down curtains. I threw food. I was skinny because the favorite punishment was locking us in the bedroom with a bucket and one meal a day. It didn't leave marks for the social workers to see, and it broke our spirits.

We each had a room and people came to 'visit' us. They paid money to spend time with us. I think Rusha started putting something in my food, or maybe I had just given up at that point. I became lethargic and mentally removed from my life. I felt like I was outside my body, just watching or refusing to watch most of the time.

My pony came then. Whenever I felt so lost that I didn't want to breathe, he came and nuzzled me. I could feel him then, and I could sleep when he was there.

I counted the years and weeks and days until I was eighteen. When that day came, I let Rusha know. She was in the lunchroom, watching us eat. I was as tall as her by then. I walked up to her and slapped her hard in front of all the kids. She punched me. I thought my nose was broken.

She said, "What do you think you are doing?"

"I'm leaving. I'm eighteen and you can't keep me here any longer."

"We will see about that," she said, dragging me by my

195

hair through the door and into the hallway. "You can't leave until you pay me what you owe me."

I grabbed the doorframe of the door she was pulling me through, but she was strong.

"I don't owe you anything," I cried as she dragged me through the door.

She threw me into another room. "You owe me the $1,000 it cost to get you. You will earn that and make a trade. Then you can go."

So I stayed long enough to earn another $1,000, doing more 'special things' for her visitors.

Then I said I was leaving. She said I still had to make a trade!

I didn't understand her until she told me to go get my sister. She said that she knew where my sister was, and that they were going to take her anyway, so I should give the $1,000 to my mother. Otherwise, they would take my sister anyway, and my mother would get nothing.

I thought my head would explode when I looked into Rusha's cold and vacant eyes. I had no choice.

I took the money to my mother. Rusha's thugs drove me to my mother's house in her Cadillac, and I gave my mother the money.

Enola was 10 years old.

18 - CAPTIVE

Irene 's face was white. She looked drained. She had told her story without emotion, with her hands wrapped tightly around her coffee cup.

I reached across the table and covered Irene's hands with mine.

"It's over," I said. "Cyra forgave you. Forgive yourself."

Irene looked down at my hands. Probably the only other women who had ever touched her with love was her mother, Cyra and Joey's mother.

I removed my hands. "So you were free. What did you do then?"

Irene shook her head. "I wasn't free." Irene continued her story:

We took Enola to that hellhole, and I thought I could just leave. But when I grabbed my little suitcase of belongings and tried to leave the car, the man sitting in the passenger seat in front of me grabbed my arm.

"Stay in the car!" he said as he pushed me back in the seat.

I tried to pull away, but he laughed and said, "Try it."

I tried to open the back doors from the inside of the car, but he just laughed. They were locked from the outside. I couldn't jump out. I was trapped.

I knew it was hopeless. My spirit was broken. I stayed in the back of the car as I was told, and the second man drove. I never knew their names.

We drove for two days. I didn't know where we were going, but I knew we were traveling across state lines because I could read the road signs: "Welcome to Utah, Welcome to Colorado, Welcome to Kansas, Welcome to Missouri, Welcome to Illinois, Welcome to Indiana, Welcome to Michigan."

We stopped only once for the night. That night, they tied me to the bed. I couldn't escape. They wouldn't let me out of their sight, even to use the restroom. They checked to make sure there were no windows in every restroom we stopped at before they let me use it and there was always one of them waiting outside the door.

Once a man questioned them. They told him I was their sister. That I had run away, and they were taking me back home. They said I had mental problems, and the man backed off.

I shook my head. "So, where did you wind up?"

"Here. Well, not here in the suburbs. In Detroit. They sold me to a judge."

I sat straight up in the booth when Irene said that. "What?"

My mother appeared at the table with 2 fresh cups of coffee. "I know these are cold," she said, taking the 2 cold cups off the table. "Do you girls want anything else?"

"Not me, Mom. Irene?"

"No, but thank you," Irene said.

"Well, okay. I'm leaving for the afternoon. If you need anything else, Jennie will be watching your table and she will get whatever you need. Your bill has been paid." My mother winked at me.

I smiled, "Thanks, Mom. I love you."

My mother smiled and turned to Irene. "It was nice to meet you," she said.

Irene smiled and nodded. "Same here."

I watched my mother walk away. My heart tugged at my chest, and I sighed.

Irene wrapped her hands around the new cup, grateful for its warmth, and continued her story:

It was okay for a while. He started out being a 'nice guy'. He bought me clothes, books, a TV, and put me in a studio apartment. It was one room with a kitchenette on one side and a bed on the other. I had a window. It didn't open, but it looked out on a rooftop three stories up. That made the room feel bigger.

I was basically locked in the little studio apartment. I had a windowless bathroom with a door that locked from the outside, but not the inside. The same was true of the front door. It was locked from the outside, too. There was always a man stationed outside my door. There were three or four of them. I didn't know their names.

The judge came to "visit" me almost every night at first. But he had political ambitions and social obligations.

He started letting other men "visit" me.

I was lonely. My pony wasn't there, and I missed having an animal. At Rusha's, place, there were dogs, but they weren't friendly. Her dogs were loyal to her and would betray us in a minute. But still, they were animals and better than humans. They didn't lie to you.

In the apartment, I had no animals until I got the cat. She just appeared at my window one day, looking at me. Just a little black cat with huge orange eyes. She rubbed her body against the windowpane and looked at me.

I put my hand against the windowpane, and she turned and rubbed her body against it. I wanted to touch her, so I grabbed a coffee cup and wrapped it in a towel and broke the windowpane. I had seen it done like that on TV with a rock wrapped in a t-shirt. It made a little noise, and she jumped away from the window, but came back in a minute.

"How did you get up here, little one?" It was three stories up. She could have fallen. But she came inside and rubbed against my legs. I stroked her and picked her up. She didn't fight, and I held her for a couple of hours. When I finally let her go, she jumped down and looked at me.

"Yes, I have food. Come and see what you like."

When the man guarding my door opened it to bring me dinner and a bag of groceries, the cat ran under my bed.

He saw the broken windowpane and laughed. "Don't try to break the panes and jump out the window," he said. "You'll break your leg." Then he pulled out his cell phone and called someone.

A man came and replaced the windowpane within the hour. Then he measured the window, wrote things on a piece of paper, and left. When he returned, he was carrying a large box. It contained a metal grid that he installed over the window and locked in place.

After the repairman left, the man guarding me said, "Don't break anything else," and he left too.

The cat came out from under the bed then. I made her a litter box and put it in the bathroom. I named her LittleBit.

Sometimes the judge took me places with him. He was running for mayor. His wife was dead, so I was presented as his secretary and fiancée. I guess he wanted to appear successful and attractive. He was careful, though. One of his bodyguards was always with us and kept an eye on me.

I met his daughter at one of these events. She was about Cyra's age. Maybe nineteen or twenty. I asked her if she liked her father. She looked at me and said, "Of course!" But then she said, "But my sister hated him."

"Oh. She doesn't hate him now?" I asked.

"She committed suicide."

I thought fast and said I was sorry, and I told her that I knew her mother had also died. She didn't seem upset, so I asked her what her mom died from. She said a heart attack.

I thought the judge might have poisoned her mother. I thought he probably killed the mother and the daughter because he was abusing the older daughter, and she told her mother. Maybe the younger daughter had also been abused. Maybe not. Maybe her older sister protected her.

I kept thinking that way and it made me angry. I didn't

know if any of it was true, but he abused me and probably the older daughter, too. Maybe he didn't abuse the younger daughter because he had me now. Maybe I had saved her. Anyway, that's what I thought.

I had to stay angry because I wanted to be free more than anything. So I just kept thinking that way and looking for the chance to escape. I had no money and no car, and I didn't have a driver's license anyway, but I wanted to be free. It was the only thing that kept me sane. I knew that, if I got the judge alone in public, without the bodyguard near, I had a chance, so I waited for the right time.

I got my chance at a fundraiser.

This particular fundraiser was held in a restaurant in Greektown. The restaurant had a large diningroom and a platform for a band. There was a small dance floor in front of the band's platform. A hallway on the left led to the rest rooms, a utility closet, and the kitchen. I knew all the exits and entrances to the building because I had been there once before with the judge for an earlier fundraiser. I knew the evening's routine too, and planned my escape.

Everything went just as it had gone before at the earlier fundraiser, so I knew what to do and when. We were slow dancing after the dinner, and I saw the bodyguard go to the front entrance of the restaurant for a quick smoke. That was the opportunity I was waiting for.

My heart was pounding as I slid the gun the judge always carried out of the hip holster under his dinner jacket and pressed it hard into his back. "Listen up, you prick," I whispered through smiling lips. "I don't care if you live or die, so it's your choice. The safety's off."

He stiffened a little, and his eyes darted around, trying to find his bodyguard.

"He's outside, having a smoke." Then I growled, "Listen to me! I know you messed up your daughter and I know she went to your wife for help, and you killed them both!"

All the blood drained from his face, and he stopped breathing for a moment. I had guessed right. But he was a clever man. He knew that cigarette break wouldn't last long. He was counting on that, so he tried to talk.

"Wait..." he said, but I cut him off.

"No!" I whispered. "You're gonna get one chance to do this right and do it now because in two minutes I'm gonna shoot you and tell everyone here that you're a murderer and that I'm your prisoner and where they can find proof of it. Right now, I'm gonna take your wallet and car keys. I'm gonna walk out of here and you will never see me again." I shoved the gun hard into his ribs and grabbed his wallet and the keys he always kept in his right pocket. Then I put the gun under my arm, released him, and headed into the hallway.

I knew the bodyguard would follow me in seconds, so I ducked into the men's restroom, I dumped the gun in the waste container and waited. Sure enough, I heard the body guard run into the hallway and enter the ladies' room.

At the same time, a man came out of a stall, zipping up his fly. I pulled my dress up and ran my hand under it. "Take me for a ride?" I whispered. He started to unzip his fly again, and I said, "Not here! Take my keys. My car's out back. It's the silver Cadillac. I'll meet you down the street at the north corner. Hurry, before my husband comes back from the bar!"

The man grinned, grabbed the keys and took off out the back door. When the bodyguard came out of the ladies' room, he ran to the back door. He heard the Cadillac start up and he opened the back door and started yelling.

The Cadillac's tires squealed as it took off. The poor man must have thought the bodyguard was my husband. When the bodyguard ran after the car, I hurried through the kitchen service door. The busy cooks didn't even look at me. I rushed through the kitchen and grabbed a coat hanging by the cook's back door. I ran down the street in the opposite direction of the Cadillac. The bodyguard had gone back inside. Probably to find the judge.

I didn't know where I was going. I just ran. I ran into Trapper's Alley. At that time, Trapper's Alley was a block long brick alley of privately owned shops three stories tall. Eventually, the property was sold, and a casino was built in its place, but back then, it was a colorful alley stacked with shops.

I ran up the stairs on my left and into a clothing shop on the second floor. I found some jeans, a t-shirt and a hip length overcoat Then I went to the cashier and paid for the clothes. I think she saw all the $100 bills in the judge's wallet when I paid for them because I asked her to call me a taxi, but she said she was getting off in a few minutes and would give me a ride.

Well, I didn't trust anyone at that point, and I thought

she might try to rob me, so I said I wanted to change first and asked if I could change in the restroom. She pointed to a door at the back of the shop.

When I came out of the restroom, the cashier said, "My relief will be her in a few minutes."

I smiled at her. "I'll wait outside."

I walked out of the store. When I was on the stairs and alone, I removed the cash from the judge's wallet and pocketed it. Then I threw the wallet into a corner of the alley. I hoped someone would find it and max out all the credit cards in it.

I got lucky. A cab was parked by the sidewalk. I got in and told the cab driver I was new in town and wanted to go to the country.

"Which country?" He squinted at me in the rear view mirror. "Canada or not the city country? What are you lookin' for, lady?"

"I just got here, and I hate Detroit. I want to be in the country and see some farm animals."

So he took me to the Armada Fair and dropped me off there.

19 - FREE

I had been holding my breath. I exhaled and sat back in the booth. "Wow…"

Irene smiled back at me, then continued her story:

I wandered around and ate from the concession stands. I petted the animals and watched some of the competitions. It felt so good to be free, and that's where I met Joey.

Joey was at a booth, talking to a man and his wife. I walked by and we kind of looked at each other. I walked on and I heard him tell the couple he had to go. He followed me. He just walked behind me, but I knew he was there.

At first, I panicked. I thought they had found me, but then I realized it was impossible. There was no way the judge could have tracked me. I didn't have a tail coming out of Detroit and the cab driver didn't know me or anything that had happened, so I relaxed. I let Joey follow me for a while, and then I turned around and said, "Why are you following me?"

"He said, 'I don't know. There's just something about you I like."

So I said, "Well, don't follow me. Show me around. I've never been here before."

And he did. We had a great time. We rode some rides. We watched the band Annabelle Road perform "Love at First

Sight" and stayed until they closed the fair for the night.

"Where do you live?" Joey asked. "I'll take you home."

I told him I had just gotten into town and that I needed to find a job and a place to stay. I told him my luggage and my purse had been stolen on the bus. I said I still had a little cash because I always kept some in my pocket instead of a purse, but I lost my driver's license and all my clothing.So I'll go to a motel tonight and look for a job and a place to stay tomorrow."

Joey shook his head.

"I don't know anyone here and I was planning on going south but, now that I've lost everything, I'll have to stay here until I figure out what to do next."

Joey grunted and looked at me. Then he said, "You can stay with my parents for a while, if you want. They could use a little help until you decide what you want to do."

"That would be great. I really appreciate it," I told him.

Joey lived in a gated community in Clinton Township. You had to identify yourself to a guard, who sat in a booth at the gate to enter, and the gates closed behind you when you went inside. Joey spoke to the guard and introduced me. He said I would be helping his parents. The guard wrote my name down.

Joey lived next door to his parents. All the relatives had houses there, like a little village. He took me to his parent's house. It was midnight and I think he woke his poor mother up. But she smiled and made coffee for us. Joey told her my story, and she said, "You can stay here. Meet Papa in the morning."

And I did. I stayed and helped her with her husband, who had muscular dystrophy, and I filed receipts and made orders for the family business from their home.

I took a deep breath. It was impossible to breathe normally while Irene was telling her story. "Did you tell Cyra? Did she finally get to know what happened and how you were used?"

"Yes, I told her during the days we spent away from the barn after we were reunited. We needed time to talk about everything and to try to get over it."

I nodded. "Did you tell Joey your story then?"

"I hadn't told him anything until then. I didn't want to lose him. He knows it all now. Cyra and I told him most of it after we talked it over."

"What did Joey say?"

"Nothing. He cried. He hugged us and cried. It was awful. And beautiful. I love him so much."

I sat back, picturing big, loud Joey crying. Men were complex. Just when you thought they were superficial, they surprised you with their depth of feeling. Like Al, I thought.

Irene relaxed her grip on the coffee cup. She tried to drink the cold coffee and choked.

Jennie heard her and came to the table.

"May we have fresh coffee?" I asked. "Irene and I talked so much, we forgot to drink our coffee and it's cold."

"No problem," Jennie said. "I'll be right back with

fresh cups."

I watched the waitress hurry away and smiled. Then I looked at Irene. "Weren't you afraid the judge would try to find you?"

"Sure," Irene admitted. "But I got lucky."

"What happened?"

Jennie returned with 2 cups of hot coffee. "Do you girls want any desert?"

"No, Thanks," Irene said.

I shook my head.

"Okay, I'll be here if you need anything else."

"Thanks," Irene said, and continued her story:

I fell in love with Joey right away. It wasn't hard to love him and his family. Joey's mom gave me a gown and a housecoat and slippers. I made breakfast for us the next morning while she got Joey's father ready for the day. We just worked together like we had always been together.

"I wanted a daughter," Joey's mother told me. "But I only had Joey. Now look. God knows what He's doing."

I think I scared Joey's mother when I started crying and hugged her. She wiped my face and said, "Stop, stop. You're gonna make me cry. Stop."

Sol helped with Joey's parents and the family business. Joey's family imports food and spices from Italy. They have 2 stores in Detroit and 3 in the suburbs. I still do that. I help by doing the books at home, accessing the inventory and making orders online.

I eventually learned how to help with Joey's father. He

is a proud man and is respected by his family. He doesn't talk much. I don't think his speech is affected much by the muscular dystrophy. He's just a quiet, thoughtful man. And he seems to like me and appreciate my help.

I ordered a few more clothes online. Just some jeans and shirts, underwear and a couple of dresses. Some tennis shoes and a nice pair of flats. I don't wear heels. I'm taller than Joey and I don't want to embarrass him.

We didn't go many places together, anyway. We spent most of our free time with his mother and father. Joey always came to their house for dinner. His mother and I cooked almost every night. Sometimes Joey would bring carry-out for us. Then we would have coffee and watch TV until bedtime and then Joey went home. His house is next door and he has a path through the hedges to his back door.

It was peaceful and safe. Until the judge came to see Joey's father.

I stopped breathing and gripped my coffee cup, "What?"

20 - THE JUDGE

Irene nodded and continued her story:

The judge was running for mayor, and I guess he wanted to get Joey's father's support with the Italian community in Detroit. Anyway, I didn't know he was there. He was sitting in the den across from Joey's father. His back was to me when I walked in the door and saw him.

I started shaking and almost dropped the tray of sweet cakes I was carrying. I managed to put one in front of Joey's father, one in front of Joey, and dropped the last one off its plate and into the judge's lap. He stood up and put the sweet cake back on the plate and handed it to me. My hand was shaking when I took it from him.

"I'll pass," he said to me.

"I'm so sorry, Judge," Joey said, getting up from his seat. "Can I get you anything else?"

"No, I'm fine, thanks," the judge said, smiling at me and brushing the crumbs off his lap and into his hand. He gestured to me and I understood that he wanted me to take the crumbs. I held out the plate, and the judge brushed the crumbs onto the sweet cake in it.

I walked to the little bar in the den's corner and put the sweet cake on the tray and tried to breathe.

Joey was watching me. "Do you want a coffee, Judge?

Or another drink?"

"No, no. I'm fine. I'll be leaving in a few minutes, anyway."

Joey nodded. "Thanks, Irene," he said.

I left the den and walked into the kitchen. I stood at the window over the sink and watched Joey's mother water her flowers in the backyard. I felt like my life was over.

I jumped when the judge came up behind me and stood so close I could feel his breath on my neck. "So," he said. "This is where you've been hiding. Good choice."

Joey walked into the kitchen and said, "Can I get you anything, Judge?" He looked at me. I had my mouth open, gasping for air. I'm sure my face was white.

The judge turned to Joey. "No, I was just leaving. Please tell your mother thank you for me. And thank your for your hospitality and the chance to speak to your father."

Then the judge put his heavy hand on my shoulder. "So nice to meet you, Irene," he said.

My knees almost gave out, and I couldn't breathe. I gripped the edge of the sink for support.

Joey walked the judge to the door and returned to the kitchen. I was still standing at the window, watching his mother water her flowers in the backyard, but tears were flowing down my cheeks.

"What's wrong?" Joey asked. He turned me to face him and wiped my cheeks.

"I need to talk to you," I said without looking him in the eyes. "Can we go to your house?"

"Of course." Joey turned and led me out the back door of his parents' house. He had his hand on my elbow, steering me through the back door and outside.

Joey's mother didn't notice us as we walked to the little path between his parent's house and his house.

When we reached the middle of Joey's backyard, he loosened his grip on my elbow and turned me to face him. He put his hand under my chin and made me look at him. "What's wrong?" he said.

I looked at him and knew that I would lose him. But I had to be honest. I owed him that much. "I haven't been totally honest with you," I said.

"What do you mean?"

"I told you I was robbed by someone on the bus, but that's not what happened."

I felt Joey's body stiffen through his hand on my elbow.

I struggled to breathe and continue, but my voice was weak, and my words came out in a whisper. "I was abducted in Nevada and sold to the judge. I was locked in an apartment in Detroit and he used me. I found a way to escape, and I ran. I wound up here with the most wonderful man I have ever met. I'm so sorry, Joey. I should have told you, but I was ashamed and afraid to lose you."

Joey grabbed my shoulders and pulled me to him. He held me for a long time and finally growled, "That sonofabitch!"

I started crying, and Joey tightened his arms around me. "You'll never lose me," he whispered.

Soon after, I heard the judge had been shot.

"What? What happened?" I asked.

"I don't know, but it was common knowledge that

215

the judge pissed off a lot of the men he sent to prison. Evidently, one of them was released from prison and heard he was campaigning for mayor. He shot him."

"Killed him?"

"No, but it left him brain damaged. I heard he can't concentrate on things, can't talk and he gets emotional. His daughter takes care of him. She has help, of course. I heard that she's spending all his money."

"Well, good for her," I said. "I suppose the gunman was caught right away? They probably knew who did it?"

"No. The gunman was never caught. Some people think it was his daughter who shot him, but she had a rock-solid alibi. She was spending the night with the chief of police of Detroit."

My mouth fell open. Then I smiled.

Irene smiled back at me. "The night the judge was shot, Joey asked me to marry him."

I took a deep breath. "Well," I said, sitting up in the booth, "we both know how that ended!"

Irene laughed. "Yes, and that's a good place to stop. We need to do lunch more often, but right now, I think we need to go see our horses?"

"I agree," I said.

21 - AT THE BARN

Back at the barn, I watched Irene brush Parcel. "Your whole demeanor is different now. Even with Parcel."

Parcel had always been an aloof, but tolerant horse. He usually ignored Irene's frustration and anger or responded to it with only an irritated twitch of his tail.

"Yes, I feel more relaxed around him now. Before, I was expecting perfection, and I was always frustrated. I know he felt it. Every time I rode him, and he didn't do what I wanted, I would get angry. Then I would spur him or use the whip." Irene sighed. "I'm so sorry, Pascal." Irene stroked her horse's neck. Pascal rolled his eye back toward her. Irene laughed and picked up her brush.

"I was never happy. But that didn't seem unusual. I haven't been happy since I was 10 years old. When I met Joey, I felt safe. He was so kind. He was patient. He protected me. It was the closest thing to happiness I had felt since I was a child. But I was still frustrated and tense around people other than Joey and his family. It was easy to take it out on my horse when he didn't do what I wanted him to do. And, of course, I was a cold bitch to everyone at the barn because I didn't know how to be open and vulnerable with anyone."

"Yes, you certainly were a bitch!" I laughed.

"Yes, but then Enola came back into my life. That changed everything."

Parcel bobbed his head, and Irene and I laughed.

"Pascal's different too. He knows you're different now."

"Yes. I'm so glad I never rode Fortunate. He's way too young and sensitive to understand. Bonnie has done a great job training him. I would have ruined him with all my issues."

Fortunate was Irene's young horse. He had been imported from Germany as a 3-year-old and had been in training with Bonnie since then. Irene hoped to ride him in Florida during the coming winter and show him the following summer if Bonnie approved. Somehow, Irene had developed patience and empathy. The horses felt it.

"So when did you get back into horses?"

"Well, it's kind of a long story. After Joey and I got back from our honeymoon in Sicily, he taught me to drive and bought me a Maserati. He said there is nothing sexier than a beautiful woman driving a Maserati. He likes it when I drive us places. It makes him proud." Irene smiled and reached for a softer brush.

"I moved into his house after we got married, and I tried to stay busy. But I couldn't find enough to do, even though I was still doing inventory and ordering for the family business. I hated being alone in that house all day, but I didn't want to complain. Joey's mother and father came over once in a while, and I would go to their house, but they didn't need me anymore since they hired a nurse to help with Joey's dad.

I was bored. It was Joey's mother who told him I needed to get pregnant or get a dog or do something else."

I handed Irene a hoof pick and took the soft brush from her.

"We tried to get pregnant, but it didn't happen. After a year of trying, Joey's mother stepped in again. She asked me what I loved more than anything in the world. I told her Joey."

I smiled. "Of course."

"Okay." Joey's mother said. "You answered right. What is it you love next?"

"I told her I loved horses. I told her I had been watching the Olympics on TV, and I wanted to ride like that."

"What?" she said. "And jump like that? No. You will hurt yourself."

"No, I want to learn dressage," I said. "I want to dance with horses."

Joey's mother looked at me kind of funny, but she said, "Okay. You can dance with horses. I will talk to Joey."

"And the next thing I knew, Joey and I were shopping for horses. He found Centerline Farm online, and we went to see Bonnie. She was training Parcel when we got there. We watched her ride, and Joey fell in love with Parcel and the rest is history."

"But Bonnie imported Parcel from Holland for herself, didn't she? Wasn't he supposed to be her next Grand Prix horse?"

"Yes, but Joey got his way. He said he would keep Parcel in training with her and pay all his expenses for her to show him through the levels. I guess Joey's offered was hard to resist, and that probably closed the deal."

I nodded. "Well, I can understand that. Money talks. Most barns are constantly in need of money. "

"That's what I hear," Irene said.

I sighed. "Well, I'm gonna go get Chimmy and get her ready to ride with you. Real can have the day off."

Irene watched Marsha walk down the aisle to get Chimmy. She put her in crossties opposite Pascal and picked up a curry comb.

Irene frowned. She ccouldn't tell Marsha why she couldn't get pregnant. She was ashamed and afraid Marsha would be repulsed if she told her it was because her uterus was so scared from abuse and the gonorrhea she contracted as a child at Rusha's house, that it would be a miracle if she ever conceived. Her only satisfaction was thinking that she might have spread gonorrhea to her abusers, even though it was never confirmed that she actually had the disease while she was in Rusha's house. At that time, her bleeding, burning and pain were all attributed to her small size compared to the adults who abused her, and no cultures were ever taken.

Irene knew Joey wanted a child, and probably more than one. She felt guilty because she was pretty sure she couldn't give him that. Fortunately, Joey was a gentleman and never expected sex from her before marriage. After he asked her to marry him, they still maintained a chaste relationship, and Irene lived with his parents until they were married.

After Irene moved into Joey's parent's house, Joey's mother noticed Irene's cramping and erratic periods. Joey's mother suggested seeing a gynecologist, and Irene picked one at random, far away from Clinton Township where they lived.

The gynecologist confirmed Irene's fears and gave her a drug called ceftriaxone. The infection cleared up almost immediately, but Irene never told Joey about the gynecologist and the sexual abuse. She was afraid she would lose him.

After they were married, Irene kept track of her periods and tried to get pregnant, but it never happened.

Irene looked at Marsha. It was easy to talk to her, but she hadn't told her everything. Maybe she could tell her more now, but not everything.

"Did Cyra ever tell you about our life in Nevada after we were abducted?"

Marsha stopped brushing Chimmy. "Not much."

Irene took a deep breath and said:

Joey didn't know anything about my life before the

judge until Cyra convinced me to tell him. So one night after dinner, we approached Joey.

"Joey," I said, "Cyra and I have something to tell you."

"Sit down, sit down," Joey said, patting the couch where he sat, watching the evening news. He clicked the TV off.

We sat. "Joey, we want to tell you the whole story. Cyra and I have had our talks, and we need to tell you exactly what happened."

"Okay." Joey opened his hands to us.

"Our mother, Gaho, was raped twice. Once, and she conceived me. My father was a light-skinned man. The second time Gaho was raped, it was by a half-breed Indian man. Then Enola was born. After Enola was born, Gaho carried a cut-off rifle, and later, a small handgun."

Joey dropped his head and opened hands. He looked at his hands and sighed.

"After Enola was born, Gaho got a job cleaning rooms and doing laundry at a motel on the highway. We rode our ponies to work and put them in a pen in the back of the motel while we worked. Our ponies had hay and water. They ate and slept while we worked. "

"Enola was a baby, and she rode wrapped in a cloth tied to Gaho's back. She slept most of the day while we worked but, as she got older, she rode with me on my pony and tried to help with the work when we got to the motel. I was ten years old when I was abducted by a man at the motel. Enola was two years old. She rode my pony to work after that."

Joey inhaled deeply and looked at us. He had tears in his eyes. I reached out and wiped his tears away.

"Enough," Joey said and took my hands in his. "And where are these people now?"

"Probably still in Nevada. Probably still grabbing children."

Joey grunted. "What city? What's the woman's name? Who are the men?"

I told Joey Rusha's name and where she lived. "I don't know the names of the men who work for her," I said. "I just know there are at least three of them."

I had been holding my breath while Irene talked. I exhaled and said, "So what happened? Is this Rusha woman still abducting children?"

"No. Two weeks later, Rusha was arrested on drug trafficking charges. She pleaded not guilty, but she was sent to prison, anyway."

"Drugs! She was selling drugs too?"

"No, I don't think she was. But the FBI reportedly received a tip about a large stash of heroin, meth and cash. They raided her house and found the drugs and cash. She was arrested, tried and convicted. She's still in prison. She has been beaten up so many times by inmates that they wound up putting her in isolation."

I frowned. "I don't understand. If she wasn't a drug dealer, what happened? How did the heroin and meth get there?"

"Strange, isn't it?" Irene said with a smile. "I think someone tipped off somebody about what she was doing." Irene raised one eyebrow at me, "and whoever got the tip decided to make it quick and clean so she would be put away for a long time. There was no mention of child abuse in the newspapers. Only that the children were underweight and socially inhibited. Maybe it was done that way to prevent anyone from knowing what she had done and copying her crimes. Or maybe it was done that way to protect the children. Anyway, the drug charge put her away for 40 years and with no chance of parole because that was her second offense. She was busted for drugs as a teenager, so she will probably be in prison for the rest of her life."

I nodded slowly and smiled at Irene. "I think I know where the tip came from. What a great way to take care of the problem! Now Rusha won't become famous and write a book or make a movie like other criminals have. She will just die as an uninteresting, lowly drug dealer."

"Exactly," Irene said.

Chimmy snorted and tossed her head as if agreeing with. Her blue roan coat looked as if it were sparkling as it flowed down to her shiny, black legs. Her long forelock, mane and tail glistened in the afternoon light.

"Chimmy looks so good," Irene said.

Chimmy blew out her nose and tossed her head again as if agreeing with her.

"Let's work on Grand Prix movements?" Irene suggested. "We could, maybe, even try a Pas de Deux?"

"Really? Do you think the world is ready for a Mutt and Jeff performance?" I asked, laughing.

"Seriously. Let's do it. Both horses are training Grand Prix. They can do it, and it will be fun!"

"Okay. Why not?"

"I'll call out directions for you. I'll be doing the same thing, either with you or opposite you."

"Okay. Cool."

After the horses were warmed up, Irene and Marsha rode together, practicing Grand Prix movements.

Marsha was still getting used to Chimmy and trying to adjust her body to the smaller, rounder horse's gaits. She was in a "zone," concentrating on nothing but her horse and her body, when Bonnie walked into the arena and stood at the rail.

Irene saw Bonnie watching them from the rail and nodded at her. Bonnie smiled back and stayed at the rail.

Irene started calling out Grand Prix movements to Marsha and did the same movements on Pascal at the opposite end of the arena. Marsha was smiling and laughing so much that Irene kept calling. When they had ridden all the movements of Grand Prix, and halted at X, Bonnie clapped her hands and startled Marsha.

Marsha laughed, and walked Chimmy over to the rail by Bonnie.

"That was very good," Bonnie said and walked into the ring. "I must say though, your dance is a little unusual!"

"Well, Marsha rode Chimmy today, and I thought

an impromptu Pas de Deux would be fun," Irene laughed.

"Impromptu? I think you had this all planned." Marsha shook her finger at Irene.

Bonnie laughed. "Well, if you two want to do a Pas de Deux, we can work on it. Although, I think mis-matched horses might call for a comic twist somewhere."

"That could be refreshing," Irene said. "It might wake up some of the judges!"

Chimmy tossed her head and blew her nose, then pawed at the arena footing.

Bonnie laughed and thought about how much everything had changed.

22 - THE LAST HORSE SHOW

It was the last Friday in September and Bonnie was loading supplies for Centerline's last horse show of the season. Since May, competitors from Centerline Farm, had shown their horses at the show grounds Waterloo, located near Jackson and this was their last opportunity to quality for awards and regional finals, which were being held at Kentucky Horse Park that year.

Even those not interested in regional finals looked forward to the last show of the season at Waterloo. For some, it was a graduation from one level to the next. For others, it was a party to celebrate the end of the season. For Irene, it was a steppingstone to the winter shows in Florida.

Irene, as in the previous years, would be leaving for four months of training and showing in Florida. Joey would fly down to Ocala to spend weekends with her, but she would miss him, her in-laws and her friends more than she admitted to anyone but me.

"Are you sure you can't come to Florida with us this year?" Irene almost pleaded with me.

"I can't. I promised Susan I would stay and help run the barn while Bonnie is gone. And I'm just not ready. I need to get to know Chimmy better this winter and work on the Forth Level movements. I'll go with you next winter, I promise."

"Okay. I'll miss you."

"No you won't You'll be too busy learning to ride Fortunate and keeping up with Bonnie. You won't miss me at all," I laughed. Then I nodded toward the trailer. "It looks like Bonnie's almost ready to load the horses. Here we go!"

Irene looked serene as she watched Bonnie organize the 6-horse trailer. They wouldn't be taking the 6-horse trailer this time since not everyone at the barn would be showing this weekend. She knew that Bonnie had already organized her own 2-horse trailer with living quarters. Bonnie always camped out with the horses at the shows.

I suddenly felt deflated, as if I was missing something. Then I had to admit that it was Layne and Cyra I was missing. Layne should be barking orders at everyone to load up the trailers for the show. Cyra should be cheerfully helping her and then driving the 6-horse trailer to Waterloo for them. But neither would be present.

Layne had been missing for 2 years, and it was doubtful that Susan would ever allow her to come back to work at Centerline Farm when she was released from prison. But, even if Susan forgave her for Cyra's death, would the boarders accept her coming back? I shook my head and tried to shake off the depression I felt. I turned and went to get Real.

It was Real's last show of the season, and I knew

he was ready. We would be showing Third Level and were schooling Fourth Level at home.

When I bought Real and moved him to Centerline, I had ridden only to Second Level. Real was trained through Third Level and schooling Forth. Bonnie immediately recognized his talent and convinced me to not hold him back. And I had to admit Bonnie was right . Learning the upper levels was easy when I rode Real, and we advanced quickly. I think the fact that his owner had not started him under saddle until he was a 4-year-old contributed to Real's soundness and good attitude.

Real was waiting in his stall, his legs wrapped and his sheet on. His halter, fitted with head-bumper protection, was hanging by his stall door. He wasn't interested in the full hay bag hanging in his stall and greeted me with a whinny that said, "Come on! Let's get this show on the road!"

I laughed and reached for his halter.

Pascal and Real loaded onto the 4-horse trailer and 2 more horses were loaded after them. The trailer would be driven to the showgrounds by Connie's husband Kevin, while Bonnie would follow them in her 2-horse with living quarters, hauling her Grand Prix horse, Bravo and Danielle's horse Woodsman.

Irene and I traveled together, following the 4-horse trailer in my new Cadillac. Joey would be driving to the showgrounds on Saturday night to watch Irene and Pascal compete. My husband, Al, was out of town as usual, working with a new client in New York.

Same 'ol, same 'ol, I thought as we followed Bonnie's trailer. Al was always working. It was good to have Chimmy. A second horse and working for Susan during the winter would keep me busy, while Al worked the same long hours he had always worked since I met him.

September in Michigan is beautiful. Days are bright and blue, and nights are cool. It's wonderful for sleeping and the cooler weather keeps horseflies and other pesky bugs to a minimum. The coming winter would reduce their numbers to zero and limit their numbers in the spring. Fall in Michigan was always a blessed relief to both horses and humans.

Two hour later, gravel crunched under my car's tires as I pulled into the showgrounds. I let Irene out at the office and drove on to park the car with the other competitor's vehicles on the grass beyond the camping area.

The stalls designated for Centerline were at the top of a small hill overlooking the show and warm up arena. I hurried to the barns to help set up the stalls and make the horses comfortable. Bonnie was unloading the trailer with Connie and her husband was bedding down the stalls, hanging hay bags and, in general, doing all the little things that kept everyone busy and not thinking about the obvious absence of Layne and Cyra.

They say time heals all wounds, but I doubted

it. I had never gotten over the loss of my grandparents and I knew I would never get over the death of Cyra. Thinking about Cyra made my throat close up, and I coughed to cover up the effect it made on my voice.

"Sorry," Kevin said. "I didn't realize these shavings were so dusty."

"It's okay," I said. "No big deal. I'll grab the hose and fill the water buckets."

After the stalls were set up, the horses were taken out for a walk around the show grounds. They had seen it all before, but each show proved that things had changed a little, and horses are always skeptical of changes. Seeing the show grounds the day before the show relaxed them a little and prepared them for the busy days ahead.

Real and Pascal walked calmly, grabbing a few mouthfuls of grass when they could, while Irene and I watched trailers being unloaded.

Irene had shown Pascal at Waterloo for 6 years and they had seen a lot of changes. The office had switched from manual recording of entries and scores to digital recordings, and the show grounds had received several improvements, including new stabling and improved show rings.

I walked Real slowly beside Irene and Pascal. The silence between us made the air feel thick, and I felt compelled to say something. "Isn't it nice to have a few hills and valleys to walk the horses on?"

"Maybe," Irene said. "I'm so used to flat grounds at

the barn and in Florida that I get a little winded walking up and down the hills here all the time."

I laughed. "And I thought I was just out of shape! When is Joey coming? Tomorrow or tonight?"

"He will be here Saturday night."

"Good. It will be nice to see him again. I'll go to dinner with everyone, but I'll be sleeping in the barn with the horses."

"You don't need to do that," Irene said, watching Pascal grab a mouthful of grass.

"Yes, I do. I used to stay with Cyra," I instantly regretted my words, "and I need to keep an eye on the horses."

Irene had dropped her head at the mention of Cyra's name, but lifted it to look at me. "Bonnie can watch the horses," she said.

"I know, but I love staying with the horses, anyway. And Barb is coming to braid them after 9. I can help her if she needs help. Bonnie will check on us and the horses a couple of times during the night."

Irene nodded and looked away, but not before I saw the glint of tears in her eyes. I sighed and ran my hand through Real's short mane.

By midnight, all the horses had been braided, re-watered, and given a flake of hay. I put my sleeping bag on top of a folding cot and set my alarm for 5 am.

At 5 I woke, hayed and grained the horses and topped off their water buckets.

Then I gagged and felt the need to vomit.

Bonnie arrived at 6:30 and found me behind the barn, gagging. "You're pregnant," she said.

"What? No, I just ate something that disagreed with me."

"No," Bonnie shook her head and laughed. "You're pregnant."

My hand went to my belly. I had missed my last period, it was true. Maybe Bonnie was right.

"Give it an hour, then eat something," Bonnie said.

"Okay. But it's hard to imagine eating anything right now."

"Trust me," Bonnie laughed. "In an hour, you will be starving."

And I was. Connie, Kevin, Danielle and Irene met us for breakfast at 7 and Bonnie said, "Are you going to tell them the good news?"

Connie, Kevin and Irene looked at me.

"Well, I'm not sure," I said, "but Bonnie thinks I'm pregnant."

"Wow, congratulations," Connie said, laughing.

"Awesome," Kevin said.

Irene stared at me in silence. The one thing she wanted more than anything was to give Joey a child. She was jealous.

Before I could react to Irene, a waitress appeared, and all eyes turned to her. "Hi. My name is Linda and I'll be your server. Are you ready to order?"

"We're starving!" Bonnie said and everyone laughed

except me and Irene.

The first day of the horse show was quiet. Everyone was missing Cyra and Layne, but no one said it. It had been that way all summer. The horses performed well, but they also seemed subdued. Cyra used to spend the night with the horses, as I was doing now, and she would re-braid and touch up horses' braids for their owners. But now, all the horses kept their braids intact overnight and did not need touch-ups.

The twins were missing too, along with their light, comical presence. Ben and Martin, had graduated from college in June and immediately headed to Florida to pursue their dream of opening a dinner theater with horses.

Joey had joined Saturday afternoon. Irene rode well and Joey clapped loudly as she exited the arena. Irene blushed and jumped off Pascal and hugged her husband. Pascal started to walk away, but Bonnie grabbed his reins.

Bonnie and I walked Pascal back to the barn while Joey and Irene followed behind.

"Hey, hey, Bonnie!" Joey called out to Bonnie, even though she was right there, walking in front of him and Irene. "Dinner at the Meadows tonight?"

"Yes," Bonnie answered. "Same as usual. 7 pm."

"Good, good," Joey answered. Then he turned to me and fist-bumped my shoulder. "Irene told me you are pregnant!" Joey boomed. "Congratulations!"

Irene looked at the ground as she walked beside Joey.

"Yes, maybe. Bonnie thinks so, anyway," I joked, hoping Irene would smile..

"Wonderful!" Joey turned to Bonnie again. "Okay. We gotta go. Bonnie, you will take care of Pascal for us? Irene and me, we gotta go make a baby before dinner, okay?"

Bonnie laughed, "We got you covered, Joey! Go make a baby."

Irene blushed and, for a minute, I thought she might start to cry. But when Joey picked her up and swung her in a circle, she laughed.

Sunday morning brought more gagging, and I covered my mouth when Bonnie caught me behind the barn again.

"It won't last forever," Bonnie said. "Give it a couple of weeks. Your body is just adjusting to the fact that a little person is growing inside you."

"Well, I wish it would adjust some other way," I groaned. "This is a drag, gagging and feeling sweaty for a half hour each morning." And frightening, too, I thought. A person growing inside my body? And how did Bonnie know so much about pregnancy?

By 8, I was feeling ravenous. But I had a class at 8:30, and there was no time to eat. Feeling weak, I brushed Real and saddled him. After that, I felt a little stronger and led him out to the warm up ring. After 10 minutes of warm up, I felt much better and began to smile again.

Bonnie had been watching me. "You look good," she said and handed me my dress coat. "Adjust your tie a little to the left. Good."

"Thanks," I smiled down at Bonnie.

Bonnie wiped my boots and Real's mouth. "Good to go," she said, and I headed to the show ring at the bottom of the hill. By the time I got there, I felt excited and eager to be entering the ring once again on my dream horse.

By the end of the day, blue, red and yellow ribbons hung from the line across Centerline tack stall. Bonnie stood back and looked at them. "Not bad, not bad," she said.

"Damn good, I'd say." Kevin reached out and hugged Connie.

"Well, let's go get cleaned up and eat a big dinner," he said. "Joey and Irene are meeting us at the bar at the Meadows."

Bonnie turned to me. "No drinks for you, lady!"

I groaned. "I can't drink, I'm getting fat and I want to throw up every morning. I'm glad pregnancy lasts only 9 months."

Bonnie patted me on the back. "You won't have morning sickness much longer."

"Well, that's good news."

"Yeah, but you will have a totally different body soon..."

"Great. Just what I wanted to hear." I forced myself to smile, but I really didn't feel like smiling. I wanted to ask her how she knew so much about pregnancy, but there were too many people standing around.

Sunday was the last day of the horse show. The last day of any show is somber, but the last day of the last horse show was even more so for Centerline Farm that year. Adding to their sadness in missing Cyra, Layne, and the twins was the fact that dressage was slowly changing from classical to show ring dressage.

In the past, all competitors looked alike and rode to the guidelines of classical dressage, passed down through the years from great horsemen to grateful students. In the past, all competitors wore black coats, white breeches, and black boots. Short coats and hunter-type helmets were worn at the lower levels and tailcoats and top hats were proudly worn at the FEI levels. All horses wore black saddles, white saddle pads and a plain black bridles.

Now that had changed, although the change was happening a little slower in Michigan, due, in part to the fab four: Chuck Grant, Vi Hopkins, Lillian Zimmerman and Major Robert Borg, all stern advocates of classical dressage, and all hailing from Michigan.

Although sometimes accused of performing circus dressage, Chuck Grant was the loudest advocate of classical dressage. Chuck brought dressage to the Midwest after serving in the 122nd Field Artillery in the US Army, judged the first American Dressage show in the states and trained 17 horses to Grand Prix.

He was also a member of the American Horse Show Association, and a founding member of the United States Dressage Federation and the Midwest Dressage Association. In addition, he wrote 4 books and several articles on dressage. For that, he became known as the Father of American Dressage.

Chuck Grant's second wife, Carol Grant of Oxford, Michigan, competed in the World Equestrian Games, Olympic Festivals and Can-Am Challenges, and won two gold medals in the 1983 Pan-Am Games. She also trained in Germany for the Olympics.

Although classical dressage riders competed against each other at shows in the past they were really competing against themselves, measuring their ability to train their mounts by riding tests at competitions. But now, dressage was morphing into a competitive, instead of a developmental sport and the prizes were ribbons, trophies and monetary rewards in the form of client followings.

Now riders wore colorful coats and helmets and boots costing thousands of dollars. Their horses wore jewel encrusted bridles with color-coordinated saddles. Saddle pads, too, were becoming more colorful and be-jeweled. Dressage shows were becoming fashion shows.

The competitions had also become muscle events in which riders strong-armed their horses into over-bent necks pulled into their chest, stopping the development of natural collection over their backs, producing weak mimics of what should have been flowing, powerful gaits. Horses became stilted leg-movers and dressage no longer looked majestic and powerful.

All these things were being rewarded by judges who had previously given low scores for non-adherence to classical principles. At least some of the judges were guilty of that. Maybe it was because Michigan had been the home of classical dressage that the trend was slower to develop here, I thought.

Still, it was depressing to see these changes at the shows. Riders began to scratch rides with judges who scored classically and filled classes with judges who scored competitively. Horses sometimes left the arena with bloody noses and numerous spur marks, which, in the past, would have disqualified them.

Adding to my depressed mood was the fact that Irene and Bonnie would be leaving for Florida in October. I was afraid that I might, in fact, be pregnant and I would miss talking to Bonnie and Irene about it. But at least I had Susan and my mother to talk to.

I tried to make conversation with Irene during the drive home, but she was unusually quiet.

"I'm gonna miss you and Bonnie when you go to Florida," I said.

"Well, you've got a busy winter coming up,"

Irene replied. "You will be helping Susan at the barn. You're going to be riding Chimmy and Real, and you're pregnant. I envy you."

I thought Irene almost sounded angry. "And I'm scared to death about all of it," I admitted.

Irene sighed. "I would love to be scared with you. I would stay home for the winter and go through it all with you. Joey wants a baby more than anything. We've been trying to get pregnant for years. But no result. We tried going on a vacation. That's why we took a trip to Italy last month. Nothing. We have been monitoring my temperature. Nothing. Now Joey wants to go to a fertility specialist. So, I guess that's next. I would love to be pregnant with you."

"Well, I think you should relax about it. Buy another horse and it'll happen. Then you'll be too busy to think, like me."

"I tried that. Remember? Well, at least the lesson aisle got a good horse. Layne wanted to buy a farm and run it together before she went away. She said I would be so busy, I would stop worrying about it, and I would get pregnant."

"She was probably right. Are you looking for a farm now?"

"No. That was her idea. Not mine. I don't even know if I could be a good mother. I helped my mother with Cyra when she was little, but does being a big sister teach you how to be a mother?"

"I think so. I think you will make a wonderful

mother," I said, glancing at Irene's sad face.

"How about if you teach me? Tell me everything you're going through, so I'll be ready."

"Only if you agree to help me when the baby gets here. That is, if I'm really pregnant."

"For sure. You know it. I would be hurt if you didn't let me help." Irene smiled.

I wish I could tell Irene everything I'm going through. I would tell her I'm scared to death. I would tell her I feel so alone in this because Al is always gone. I would tell her I would consider abortion, but everyone seems to know now but the two most important people in my life: Al and my mother. I didn't want to, but I guess I need to tell them before they get told by someone at the barn.

"Will you let me help take care of your little one while you ride at the barn?"

"Well, of course. You can babysit anytime. My mother and Al are always working, so I really need your help."

"Perfect and if I get flustered, I can always run to the arena and get you!"

"That's true," I laughed.

When we arrived at Centerline, everyone unloaded the horses and left everything else in the trailers for the barn help to unload on Monday morning. I watched Irene drive away and, after saying hi to Chimmy and by to Real and Pascal, I climbed back in the car and headed home.

The streets of Richmond were quiet and empty of the traffic I always experienced during the week when I went to the barn, and the emptiness intensified my feelings of aloneness. In spite of the empty streets, it seemed to take forever to get to I-94, which was also devoid of the usual traffic. Sunday evening, I thought, a time to be with family. Right.

When I finally got home, I found that Al had left me a message on the recorder. He was delayed, as usual, with a client. It was no surprise, and I was alone again in their big empty house. A baby would certainly fill the loneliness.

The baby would be born in late February or early March. Irene would be back from Florida in February. I breathed a sigh of relief as I thought about it. Well, at least I had that.

I longed to call my mother, but it was too late. She would be asleep because she had to go to get up at 4 am and go to work at 5 the next day.

I sighed and poured myself a glass of wine. I looked at the dark burgundy color and swirled it in the glass. Then I remembered that I couldn't drink any alcoholic beverages while I was pregnant. I threw it it in the sink, the glass shattered, and I broke out in tears.

23 - IRENE LEAVES FOR FLORIDA

I couldn't eat breakfast the next morning. I wanted to throw up. My stomach convulsed but I could only spit a little because I hadn't eaten anything the night before.

I called my mother at work, something I had never done before.

My mother was breathless when she came to the phone. "What? What happened?" my mother said.

"Oh Mom, I'm sorry. I need to ask you something. How long does morning sickness last and will it get worse? I want to throw up every morning. I think I'm pregnant."

"Well, of course you are," my mother laughed. "And it won't last very long. Two weeks or a month. You can probably eat a couple of hours after you wake up. When did you find out?"

"I haven't yet. I got sick last weekend at the horse show and Bonnie said I was pregnant," I groaned. "Now everyone at the barn thinks I'm pregnant."

"Well, of course you are!" my mother repeated. "Don't worry. Come get some breakfast here with me. Let me see you."

"Okay, Mom. Thanks." I felt relieved. My mother would explain everything.

I got dressed, grabbed my car keys and flew out the door in 5 minutes.

October came and Irene, Bonnie and Connie left for Florida. The twins were already there and would be training with Bonnie too. The barn echoed with loneliness as Susan showed me what my barn duties would be. I would feed grain and hay each morning and supervise turnout when the barn help arrived. I would also supervise the stall cleaning and make sure water buckets were scrubbed and filled with fresh water and hay was placed in each stall according to the feed instructions on each stall door.

I would be able to ride Chimmy and Real during the day and, at the end of the day, I would supervise bringing the horses in, removing fly sheets and putting on stall sheets. In my spare time, if there was any, I could clean the observation room.

"Thanks so much for the help," Susan told me.

"It's no problem," I said. "I need something to do to keep my mind off the pregnancy. It's all new and, frankly, I'm scared."

Susan smiled. "I know how you feel. When I got pregnant with Bonnie, I was totally unprepared for what was coming. And then, when I had to be bed ridden for the last months of the pregnancy, I almost lost my mind. I understand how confusing and lonely you must feel. I know you have your mom, but if you ever want to talk to me about anything, I'm always here for you."

"I really appreciate that, Susan. I'm sure I will be bothering you with a dozen questions soon. Thanks." I hugged Susan and felt a little better.

Susan paid me by covering the board on Chimmy and Real each month, although I would have worked for free, just to keep my mind off the pregnancy.

"Bonnie will be back in February. You're due in February right? I can take over your chores when it gets to be too much. Don't worry about anything," Susan told me.

"That's okay. I'll be fine."

Susan looked doubtful, and I thought about the fact that Susan had been bedridden during the last months of her pregnancy with Bonnie. I quickly put that out of my mind. I didn't think I could endure that.

I still hadn't gone to a doctor, in spite of my mother's urging, which eventually turned into nagging.

"Really, Mom. What will the doctor say? You're pregnant and you're doing fine? I know that. But I guess you're right. I'll need vitamins or something soon. Will you go with me? I'm scared."

"Of course, I will. Just schedule it on my day off?"

"Yep. Thanks, Mom. I will."

I was relieved. After all this time, I still felt I needed my mother to guide me and hold my hand. I wondered how Irene could cope without her mother but I thought Joey's mother would fill that vacancy.

I made the doctor appointment for a Wednesday,

my mother's day off, and let Susan know I wouldn't be at the barn that day.

"Good," Susan said. "Let me know if you need any more time off. I can fill in for you."

I made the appointment for 9 am and picked up my mother at 7:30. We drove to Port Huron and had a quick breakfast at a restaurant recommended by Susan. Thankfully, my morning sickness had stopped.

As I predicted, the doctor found nothing unusual and prescribed a vitamin supplement for me.

"Satisfied?" I asked my mother.

"Absolutely! Now let's get some baby furniture and do some baby clothes shopping!"

"Uh, Mom. I haven't told Al yet."

"What?"

"Well, I wasn't sure. And he works all the time. I didn't want to upset him."

"Marsha. It's time. It's his child. He needs to know."

"You're right. I know. I'll tell him tonight when he calls. Now that it's for sure. Now that the doctor confirmed it."

But I forgot my promise to my mother and didn't tell Al. Also, I didn't see Susan much, and Susan seemed preoccupied when I saw her. The morning sickness had stopped, and I almost forgot I was pregnant.

Until I felt the baby kick. At first, I thought I had eaten something that didn't agree with me. When my stomach did a little flutter, I tried to remember what I had eaten for lunch. I placed my hand on my stomach, thinking. And I felt it again. It was like butterfly wings beating in my stomach. Then I knew. It was the baby. It was the first time I felt it was real. Then I realized I was smiling.

I told Al that night when he called me.

"Hi, hon," Al said. "Sorry to call so late. We just got out of a meeting. How are you doing?"

"I'm fine. Al, I think I'm pregnant."

"What?"

"I'm pregnant. I went to the doctor and I'm pregnant."

"Wow... I don't know what to say. How are you feeling?"

"I'm scared."

Al chuckled. "Me too. But I'm thrilled. I'm going to be a dad. Wow. I'll be home in two days. I love you."

"I love you too." I knew he was saying goodnight. "Goodnight," I said.

Al was still working all the time and traveling all over the United States for his clients. I wondered how I would be able to raise a child by myself. I was scared.

24- NO MORE RIDING

During this time, I spoke to Irene more than I spoke to Al. Irene called me every night, and sometimes during the day. But she didn't call when Joey was with her. Irene didn't want to talk about babies when Joey was around. I understood and waited patiently until Monday to hear from her again.

"Hi Marsha. What's new?"

"I felt the baby move. I finally went to the doctor, and he said I was four and a half months along. He said I should have felt the baby move sooner, but I probably just ignored it. Anyway, I got some vitamins, and I'll see him again in a month or two. I told Al last night."

"What did Al say?"

I laughed. "He's scared. At least he was honest. I'm scared too, but I'm more scared of doing this alone than I am of being pregnant."

"You're not alone," Irene said. "I'm right there with you anytime you need me. Including now. I'll fly home if you want me to. Just say the word."

"No, no. I'm fine. Just lonely. I'll be okay until you get home. Thanks."

"Okay, but the offer stands. Joey left last night. I miss him already. I don't know how you do it without Al being there with you."

"Yeah, I get really lonely and afraid."

"I'm sorry. I shouldn't have said that. Do you want me to fly home now? I'll do it..."

"No, honestly, I'm good. You'll be home soon enough."

Irene sighed. "I wish it was me."

"Yeah, I wish it was you, too. Night. Talk to you tomorrow." I disconnected before Irene could realize I was crying.

"Goodnight." Irene was crying too.

I was in my 5th month of pregnancy, and my body was changing dramatically. My belly was bulging, and I found it impossible to sleep on my stomach. When I slept on my side, I had to use a small pillow to get comfortable. Every morning, my legs and feet were swollen. I decided to ease up on salt and spices. To make matters worse, it was getting harder to sit properly in the saddle, and Susan urged me to stop riding.

"I'll be okay. Riding is good exercise," I laughed.

My doctor wanted me to stop riding too, but I refused to quit. Al hadn't said anything. He called on a regular basis when he was out of town, but he didn't seem to worry about the riding. Or he didn't realize that I was still riding.

I rode until I was 8 months pregnant. I rode in the stretchiest yoga pants I could find, but they were slippery, and I felt awkward in the saddle. So I gave up riding in a saddle when the pommel started hitting my belly. Even though riding bareback in yoga pants was slippery, Chimmy and Real seemed to know I was pregnant and moved carefully. When I had to grip with my legs to keep my balance, they didn't react. But by then, I wasn't doing more than a collected canter.

Nevertheless, Susan and Irene breathed a sigh of relief when I quit riding. My mother just nodded, knowing her opinion wouldn't matter. Al was still gone a lot and seemed oblivious to the changes in my body and my daily life.

In bed at night, struggling to get comfortable, I put my hand on my enlarged belly and cried. I didn't want to be pregnant, and I couldn't tell anyone how I felt. I was ashamed. So many people wanted babies, and I was lucky enough to have a healthy pregnancy and a husband who could afford the best for our child. I had a supportive mother and good friends. But I couldn't tell anyone how I felt.

It wasn't fair. I didn't want to be pregnant. Not yet. It was too soon. I needed more time to achieve my goals in life. Then the time would be right for children. How did I let this happen?

The baby was growing. It was taking over my body. Now it would move under my ribs and kick several times a day. I was uncomfortable and unable to fix it. I felt possessed by an alien creature who was taking over my life.

The days dragged on. Every morning, I went to the

barn and fed the horses. I walked the horses out to the pastures with the barn help, and I supervised the stall cleaning. The middle of my day was filled with putting hay in the stalls, cleaning the observation and tack rooms, and walking outside to bring the horses back in.

My life and my days had been confiscated. They were no longer mine. Soon, I told myself, I'll get my life back.

I wondered how my mother felt when she was pregnant. I remembered my mother saying only that she was depressed when she lost her first child. Then, when she had me, she had gave up everything to raise me in a safe environment.

I felt selfish and ashamed. I wondered if I was harming the baby with my negativity. But it wasn't fair. I didn't want to be pregnant.

I missed the next doctor's appointment because I felt that monthly appointments were unnecessary. When I went to see him the following month, he insisted on an ultrasound to check the health of the baby.

My mother was with me, and we watched the screen in the doctor's office. My mother smiled at the ultrasound, but I frowned and said, "How can you tell anything from those images? How do you know if the baby is healthy?"

The nurse smiled patiently and said, "I can read an ultrasound after seeing so many. Do you want to know what sex your baby is?"

I shrugged, "I guess so..."

The nurse smiled again. "It's a girl," she said.

"Good," I said. Now I knew what color clothing to buy.

"Do you have any names in mind?" the nurse asked, making conversation.

"No, I hadn't thought about it."

"Well, we have lots to talk about," my mother said.

After the ultrasound, we went back to the doctor's office. "If you have any discomfort, call my office immediately," he said.

I nodded.

"We can always do a C-section."

My eyes flew open. "That won't be necessary."

"I hope not. When you are in labor, we will give you a spinal, so you won't feel any pain."

"I want a natural childbirth," I told him. "I walk all day and before I rode every day, so I want to have a natural childbirth."

"Okay," the doctor patted my knee, "we will see when the time comes."

I felt a sudden surge of anger. The doctor was treating me like a child. Or a silly woman. I was insulted, but I bit my tongue.

I called Al that afternoon. He called back 3 hours later.

"Hi, hon. How are things? How is the baby? Did

you see the doctor lately?"

"Yes. We're having a girl." I remembered to tell him.

"Great! Let's think of a name soon, okay?"

"Sure. The doctor said I'm due in middle or late March."

"I should be home then," Al said.

"That would be wonderful, but I understand if you can't make it." I he secretly doubted Al would be in town for his daughter's birth.

"I'll be there," Al said.

Finally, February came, and Irene and Bonnie were coming home. Bonnie was driving the horse trailer back from Florida, but Irene was flying. She told me she couldn't be at the barn until the day after she got back.

"I miss you, girl, but I have another doctor's appointment when I get back, so I can't be at the barn until the next day."

I laughed. "I miss you, but I'll survive. See you soon."

Bonnie arrived at the barn on Tuesday during the first week of February. She had driven the trailer straight through from Florida, and she was exhausted. She hugged me. "How are you doing?" she asked.

"I have more energy than you,!" I joked.

With Susan's help, we unloaded the horses and left the trailer for the barn help to unload and clean the next day.

"So, I guess I'm fired now?" I asked Susan.

"Not unless you want to be," Susan replied. "We can use your help until you don't want to be here."

"Then I'll see you tomorrow," I smiled and turned to Bonnie. "Get some rest."

"You too," Bonnie laughed and put up two fingers.

Irene came to the barn early the next morning. After giving me a long, silent hug, she pushed me away. "How are you feeling?"

"Everybody wants to know how I'm feeling," I grumbled. "I'm pregnant and I feel pregnant. I'm fat, grumpy, and I don't want to be this uncomfortable in my own body."

"I wish it was me," Irene said sadly.

"I wish it was too. No luck so far?"

"No, we keep trying. Taking my temperature, checking the days off on a calendar, going to doctors. We're going to go see a fertility specialist now that I'm back."

"That would be wonderful," I said. "It would be great to have another mother to talk to."

Irene laughed. "I would love it. How is Al coping with the idea of being a father?"

"I don't really know. He doesn't say much. He's still working all the time. No time to think about it, I guess."

"Men are so strange," Irene said. "When that baby

gets here, he had better wake up. It's a whole new world."

"Yeah. I'm already in that world."

"Well, let's go get smelly and brush some horses? That world is still the same and we love it."

A week later, Irene told I that she and Joey had gone to see the fertility specialist. Joey had urged the doctor to rush their results, and they got the results that morning.

"Joey is fertile, and I am too!" she told me. "The doctor will implant Joey's sperm in me at the next appointment. I'll get pregnant for sure then!"

I hugged Irene. "I'm so glad. I need company on this journey."

"You got it, girl!" Irene fist bumped me. "I'm getting implanted as soon as I ovulate."

"When is that?"

"It should be this week. I have to take my temperature, and when the time is right, we have to get in to the doctor's office right away."

"Well, good luck. Keep me posted."

"Will do."

25 - CHILDBIRTH

I was uncomfortable. I felt the baby move less now that she was bigger. I was uncomfortable sitting and couldn't sleep on my back anymore. When I tried to sleep, I had to lie on my side. When I stood up, I had to lean forward to avoid getting a cramp in my back. Sometimes I felt short of breath, and that scared me.

But when I woke at 2 am to go to the bathroom and intended to return to bed, I instead felt compelled to walk in circles, bent at the waist. Finally, after walking in circles for an hour, I called my mother.

"Mom, I know it's early, but I think I'm in labor. I can't straighten up and I can't sleep. I've been walking in circles for an hour. I'm gonna call Irene and ask her to take me to the hospital."

"Okay, I'll call Al's cell. Just get to the hospital right away. Don't come get me. I'll call a cab."

"Okay."

I called Irene and woke her up. "I'm sorry to wake you, but I think it's time. I can't sleep or straighten up. All I can do is walk in circles."

"I'll be right there," Irene said. "Get a bag together if you can. I'll be right there."

Joey was awake and listening. "I'll get the car," he said.

Al was in Ohio. My mother called his cell phone. Al answered, groggy, on the 7th ring.

"Hello?"

"Al, it's me, Marsha's mother. She's on her way to the hospital. We think the baby's coming."

"I'll catch the next flight and go directly to the hospital," Al said.

"I'll see you at the hospital." my mother hung up without saying goodbye. Then she called a cab and met Irene and Joey in the hospital's waiting room. She nodded at Joey and looked at Irene. "How is she?"

"Okay. Stable. You can go in and see her." Irene pointed a the door of across the hall.

I was sitting up in bed, my hand on my big belly.

"How are you?" Mother asked, frowning.

"Okay. Probably a false alarm. I'm sorry to get you out of bed."

"Don't be silly," Mom said and patted my hand. She touched my belly. "Is the baby moving?"

"Not much. Not much room to move in," I laughed. "and I have a bizillion stretch marks."

"Those will heal," my mother said.

Irene walked in the room and sat on the opposite side of my bed. "Al just called me. His plane landed, and he's catching a cab."

I frowned. "It might be a false alarm because nothing's happening right now. I feel awful getting everyone out of bed."

"Don't be silly," Irene said. "I want to experience

everything with you. I'm so jealous I could cry!"

And I would change places with you in a minute, I thought. "How did the fertility visit go? You went yesterday, right?"

"Yes. I'm inseminated. Now we wait."

"Good luck. I hope you're pregnant," my mother said.

"We will find out soon, I guess," Irene said, grinning.

Al arrived at the hospital a half hour later. He rushed into the hospital room, past my mother, and went to my side. He hugged me and kissed my cheek. Then he put his hand on my belly.

"How's our little girl?" he asked.

"Quiet for once," I said with a tired laugh. "I'm so glad you're here. You must have run every red light, you got here so fast."

"I did. My wife's having a baby." Al turned to my mother. "Thanks for calling me," he said.

My mother nodded and smiled. "It's good to see you. I don't get to see you much."

"That will change," Al said. "I'm going to quit the firm and start a private practice. I want to be home with my family as much as possible."

I sighed, and a tear ran down my cheek.

Al saw it and wiped it away. "I'm sorry I haven't been around much," he said. "That will change."

Then we waited. And waited. My mother decided

to go to the cafeteria and get something to eat. Irene and Joey went with her. Al stayed with me, and that's when my water broke.

"Get the doctor," I said to Al, frowning. I was scared and couldn't breathe.

Al ran into the hallway and stopped a nurse. "My wife's water broke. Is the doctor here?"

"No, I don't think he is," the nurse said. "I'll check."

Al returned and the nurse brought a young doctor into the room. He examined me and said, "She's dilated 8 cm."

He left the room.

"What's that mean?" Al said.

"I think it means you're gonna be a daddy," I said.

The doctor returned with the nurse.

Al stood up and said, "What's happening?"

"You're the husband?" the doctor said.

Al nodded.

"Your wife is having a baby."

"I know that," Al said impatiently. "When is the question."

"Soon. You can stay or leave," the young doctor said. "It's up to you."

"I'm staying," Al said and grabbed my hand.

Roll over on your side, please," the doctor told me.

I rolled over to face Al still holding my hand. I felt the doctor insert a needle into my spine.

I jumped and sucked in some air. "What was that?"

"I gave you a spinal. Soon, you won't feel any pain,"

the doctor replied.

"I wanted a natural childbirth," I said, almost crying.

"You will be awake," the doctor said, "but you won't feel any pain."

I instantly fell asleep and, when I woke up, Al was standing over me

"Good. You're awake," he said and brushed my hair away from myforehead. Then he bent down and kissed me.

"What happened?" I said.

"You had a baby. You slept through everything!" Al said, laughing. "The doctor said he had never seen such an easy childbirth!"

"Oh," was all I could say. I was stunned and angry. I felt cheated. I wanted to be awake and have a natural childbirth. I had exercised, walked and done everything right. And it was all gone now. The doctor had taken it away from me. I had slept through it.

"Where's my baby? I want my baby," I said to Al, tears forming in my eyes.

"Hang on. I'll get the nurse to bring her," Al said. He jumped up and went into the hall, looking for the nurse. He returned in a few minutes and was relieved to see that I had stopped crying. But I was still angry.

"I was here," Al said. "I saw the baby's birth. I held her after she was born." Al had moist eyes, but he smiled at me. "It was miraculous. I've never seen anything like it. It was a miracle."

I blinked, and my throat closed up. I had missed everything.

The nurse walked in with a bundle in her arms. She walked to my bed. "She has hair," she said quietly. "She doesn't look like a newborn at all. She looks wonderful. No redness, no scrunched-up face."

I reached for the bundle and the nurse lowered the bundle onto my chest.

I pulled the blanket away from my baby's face and held my breath. The nurse was right. She was beautiful.

The baby moved her head toward me, but didn't open her eyes. "Is she okay?" I asked, frowning.

"She's perfect," the nurse said. "She's beautiful and perfect."

I pushed the blanket back further and the baby's hand appeared. I touched her hand, and the baby wrapped her fingers around my finger.

"Oh, she's so tiny, amd she's so strong," I whispered.

"Yes, she's perfect." The nurse smiled at me and turned to Al. "Do you need anything else?"

"No, thank you," Al replied without taking his eyes off the baby. "I've got everything I need right here."

"Okay. I'll check on you in a half hour," the nurse said.

The baby released my hand and turned her face to my breast. I lowered my gown and put my nipple near the baby's lips. The baby bumped into it and opened her mouth. She latched onto mys nipple and suckled.

"I didn't know you were going to breast-feed," Al said.

"I didn't either," I said and sighed. "It just felt right."

Al watched for a while, then said, "I can't believe I'm a father."

I looked at him but said nothing.

"I'm gonna give notice to my firm this afternoon. I'll open my own practice and be home with my family every night."

I stopped breathing.

"I'll be home every night and weekends," Al repeated.

"Are you sure you want to do that?" I said. Can we afford it?"

"It will be okay. There's always a lot of work for a good lawyer," Al said, touching the baby's full head of hair. "Do we have a name? What are we gonna call her?"

"I want to name her Amy. It means 'to be loved.' Is that okay?"

"That's perfect," Al said. "What about a middle name? Did you think of one?"

"You decide," I said.

When my mother and Irene and Joey returned from the cafeteria, the baby was sleeping.

Irene bent down to look at the baby, and I smiled. "Her name is Amy," I said. "It means 'beloved.' Al is gonna choose a middle name."

"I'm so jealous, I could spit," Irene laughed.

"Well, get ready because I'm breast-feeding and I'll

need your help when I go to the barn."

"What? I didn't know you were gonna breast-feed. How will that work?"

"I'll have to use a breast pump and leave you a couple of bottles when I'm at the barn," I said.

"Oh! Okay. I'm so relieved!" Irene exhaled and Joey laughed.

"She's beautiful," mymother said.

"Save Wednesdays for us, Mom. I know that's your only day off, but unless you have a doctor's appointment or something like that, save Wednesdays for us."

"Absolutely," my mother said, smiling.

"Okay, we're gonna leave you now," Joey said. He went to Al, shook his hand and hugged him. "Congratulations."

Al nodded. "Same here. I'll see you more often now. I'll be starting my own law firm in this area. I want to be home with my family."

"That's good," Joey said. "Good, good."

26 - IN THE BARN AGAIN

I was in love agaim. Amy's birth had changed everything in my life. My house was filled with noise and diapers. Al was home every night, and every day, the baby did something new.

I told Al everything Amy did when he came home at 6 each evening.

"Amy tried to talk today. I think she is trying to say Da-da," I teased him.

"More like Ma-ma," Al said, grinning.

Irene became a regular visitor. She insisted on holding the baby and asked to feed her and change her diapers.

"I need to practice," she told me.

"When will you find out if you're pregnant?" It had been a month since Irene had been inseminated.

"Soon, I hope. Waiting is killing me! I'm actually getting stomach cramps, waiting."

"Is Joey getting stomach cramps, too?" I teased.

"No, thank goodness," Irene laughed. "How long will it be before you can come back to the barn?"

"My doctor thinks I should wait six to eight weeks before taking her out in public."

"Good to know. Well, you have maybe four weeks to go. I'll get lots of practice in by then," Irene said.

"Yep, and it looks like you'll get some now," I said and held Amy out to Irene. "She needs changing!"

Six weeks passed quickly, and I decided not to wait 2 more weeks. I was back at the barn the following day.

I held the baby in the front of Real and Chimmy's stalls. Both horses stretched their necks out slowly and sniffed at the baby. They jumped a little when she surprised them with a squeal and a giggle. Real snorted and shook his head, and Chimmy blew softly at her.

"Real and Chimmy don't seem to be holding a grudge about my absence from the barn," I said to Irene.

"Yes, and they are fascinated by the little creature in your arms," Irene said, rubbing her stomach.

"Cramps again?"

"Yes, I don't know if I'm eating the wrong things, or if I'm pregnant, or trying to start my period. I hope I'm pregnant."

"Has it been long enough to tell if you're pregnant? You said it took a few weeks."

"We won't know for a few more weeks," she said. "My period hasn't come yet, but it has always been irregular. I hope I'm pregnant."

I smiled. "I hope so too. Will you watch Amy? I want to brush these two and remind them of who I am."

"I certainly will," Irene said, reaching out for the

baby. "We'll be upstairs in the observation room. Take your time."

I put Amy in her open arms. "Here, get some more practice. And thanks."

"No problem."

When Irene took the baby to the observation room, I felt suddenly empty. For months, my life had been dominated by the existence of this tiny creature, who, now that I knew her, I couldn't imagine living without her. I almost ran to the observation room, but Real put his head over my shoulder and reminded me why she was at the barn.

"Hi, big fella! I missed you. And Chimmy."

Hearing her name spoken, Chimmy picked up her head and looked in my direction.

"Yes, I missed you too. I'm glad Susan let you stay next to Real. I'm glad you two have each other."

Chimmy picked up a mouthful of hay and waved it at me and made me laugh.

An hour later, I washed my hands and arms in the barn's restroom and went upstairs to the observation room. Amy was asleep in her bassinet and Irene was seated next to her, bent over and moaning.

I knelt down and covered Irene's balled up fists with my hands. "Irene! What's wrong? What's happening?"

Irene looked up with tears in her eyes, and I saw that she was also sweating and gasping for breath.

"Hold on, Irene. I'm calling an ambulance."

In minutes, the Richmond siren sounded and a few minutes after that, an ambulance pulled up to the barn.

I ran downstairs to meet them.

"In the arena or outside?" the ambulance driver said.

"Here. Upstairs in the barn," I answered and led the way to the observation room.

The driver helped Irene down the stairs and into the ambulance, and I grabbed the bassinet with the still sleeping baby in it. I jumped in my car broke the speed limit following the ambulance to the emergency room at Mercy Hospital in Port Huron.

On the way, I called Joey. "Joey, it's Marsha. I'm following the ambulance to Port Huron Mercy. Irene's in trouble. I don't know what's wrong. Meet us there if you can." Then I hung up. Thankfully, Amy was still asleep in the backseat.

At the hospital, I parked by the emergency room door and rushed in with the sleeping baby. Irene was in one of the curtained rooms, being examined by a doctor and his assistant.

Ignoring all rules and possible contamination, I ran down the corridor and pushed aside the curtains hiding Irene and the doctors.

"What's wrong with her?" I demanded.

"She needs immediate surgery, the doctor told me. Are you her sister?"

"Yes, and her husband is on the way," I said.

"Is that a baby?" the young doctor asked. "You

can't be here if that's a baby.

"I'm here," Joey said and pushed past the curtains.

I ignored the doctor and listened while the older doctor explained what was happening.

"I'm afraid she has an ectopic pregnancy and needs immediate surgery to remove the fetus, which, I'm sorry to say, is already dead and making her toxic. We also need to remove a portion of her fallopian tube. I suggest a partial hysterectomy while we are at it in order to prevent future complications."

"Do whatever you think is best," Joey said. "Don't let my wife suffer."

"No-o-o," Irene moaned from the bed.

Joey went to her and pushed the hair back from her sweaty forehead. "I can't lose you, Irene," he said. "Let the doctors do what is best."

Irene looked at Joey with eyes glazed with tears and pain. "I want a baby," she said. "I want to give you a baby."

"We will figure it out," Joey said. "Let's fix this first. Please."

Irene closed her eyes and said quietly, "Okay."

Joey kissed her hand, and the doctors wheeled Irene out of the emergency room and into surgery.

It took Irene 2 months to recover from the surgery. She might have recovered sooner if she wasn't so depressed.

"I feel like a wounded animal, and I just want to

hide from the world," she told me.

"Irene! Don't talk like that," I scolded her. "Get well. There will be a baby for you and Joey. Just get well first."

I visited Irene daily and went to the barn after seeing her. It would be another month before I felt I could ride again, but I went to the barn every day during the week and placed the Amy in the bassinet on the floor with a transparent guaze covering her basinet while I groomed the horses.

Chimmy and Real watched in quiet fascination as the baby bubbled at her toys in the bassinet and kicked her feet.

When Irene finally came back to the barn, I started to ride again.

One her second day back in the barn, Irene opened the window in the observation room and looked down at me. "You're going to give me some stiff competition when I start riding again," she said, laughing.

I wrinkled my nose. "I could never look as beautiful as you on a horse, Irene."

Bonnie brought Fortunate into the arena and walked him around the perimeter. She looked up and waved at Irene.

After my short ride, I washed up and joined Irene in the observation room. Amy was sleeping and I watched her perfect lips part as she breathed.

Eventually, I turned to Irene and said, "What's next? I know you're not giving up."

Irene smiled. "Joey and I want to try a surrogate mother. I still have my ovaries. They didn't remove them, and they're still producing eggs."

"A surrogate?"

"Yes. The doctor can take eggs from my ovaries and fertilize them with Joey's sperm in a petri dish."

"A petri dish? Like in high school biology?"

Irene laughed. "Yes. Then he will implant a viable fetus in a surrogate's womb. After that, we cross our fingers and wait."

"Wow. Have you found a surrogate yet?"

"No. We're gonna start interviewing a few next week. Fingers crossed."

"How does that work?"

"Well, from what I understand, we find a surrogate we like and agree on payments. I was told that a 'down payment' will be made, and payments will be made at certain times during the pregnancy. The balance will be paid when the baby is born. It's pretty expensive."

"What if the baby isn't healthy?"

"No idea. I guess we will have to talk to the doctor about that, but I don't think it would keep Joey from accepting the baby. There's so much to think about. I'm excited and scared at the same time."

"I would be too," I said.

"I won't be here tomorrow. Joey and I are meeting with the doctor and a couple of possible surrogates."

"Well, good luck. I hope it all works out. Ask a lot of questions," I said.

"I will. I want this to happen. The sooner the better. Amy is getting older. She needs a playmate."

Two days later, Irene rushed into the observation room. Amy was asleep in the bassinet, but I jumped and almost woke her.

"I'm so excited!" Irene whispered. "We're meeting with Al tomorrow to draw up a contract for a surrogate. We chose a surrogate yesterday. After we sign the contract, the doctor will 'harvest' (Irene made quote marks with her fingers) my eggs."

"Wow. What happens after that?"

"He puts Al's sperm in with the egg or eggs, I don't know. Then we wait. If the eggs divide and start to develop into an embryo, he implants it - or all of them, I'm not sure, in her. We make the down payment when she is confirmed pregnant. And then we wait."

"Oh. That's intense. I would chew off all my nails."

"I already have."

"How do you know she will give you the baby?" I asked, remembering how I felt after the Amy's birth.

"We have a contract, drawn up by the surrogacy agency. It's legal. I don't know. I couldn't do it, for sure."

"I hope it will all work out for you."

"Me too. It's all I can give Joey." Amy stirred in her bassinet and Irene reached down and picked her up.

A week later, Irene floated into the barn, looking for

me. I was with Amy in the observation room and we were watching Bonnie ride Weygun, one of the horses she had in training.

Irene ran up the stairs to the observation room, opened the door and stopped dramatically in the doorway. "It's done," she said, spreading out her arms.

I laughed. "What's done?"

"The whole thing. She signed the paperwork yesterday and our timing was spot on. She was implanted this morning."

I jumped up and hugged Irene. "You'll be a mom soon!"

"Maybe. But, with my luck, you never know."

"Well, I agree, you've had some bad luck. Time for a change!"

27 - THE FIRST BORN

Irene and Joey's baby was born nine months later, healthy and noisy, like his dad. Joey named him Gio Luigi.

Irene and I took turns caring for the infants at the barn. Amy was toddling around and talking a little at that point, so we had their hands full. Fortunately, Amy was happy, helpful and not prone to making messes. Gio was noisy, always hungry and happy. The only time he cried was when he lost sight of Amy, but she understood him and went back to his bassinet right away.

I laughed as she watched Amy pat Gio's head to hush him. "You're a good little mama," I told her.

Amy looked at me and said, "Yesh."

I stood up and went to the observation room window to watch Irene ride Fortunate in a lesson with Bonnie. Irene was so different now. She was relaxed and rode with patience.

"Your mama is a beautiful rider, Gio," I said quietly.

So much had changed. Irene had changed. Al had changed. I had changed.

Normally, change frightened me, but I was slowly learning that change could be a good thing.

When winter came, I would finally be going to Florida to train with Bonnie. After that, the next summer I would show Real and Chimmy. The babies would also go to Florida and to the shows. So much had changed.

We are so lucky, I thought. What could possibly go wrong?

EPILOGUE

Two years passed, and the babies grew up happy and secure in their mother's horse world. They learned to sit on Chimmy and Real and be led around by Marsha, while Irene held them securely on the horse's backs. Eventually, they would learn patience and hard work, caring for their own ponies. Everything seemed wonderful...

Until Layne was released from prison on parole.

...continued in **THE HORSE CONNECTION** part 3

Loving Mother

and leaving her at any cost

"Your mother has had an accident and you need to come home."

Home. There was that word again. My shoulders dropped. Would I ever be free of this woman? Every time I thought I had gotten free, I found myself returning home again. I let out a deep sigh. I had been stupid to think that I could be free.

"Is she gonna die?" I asked.

"No, but she needs 24 hour care."

It suddenly occurred to me that I would have to be the caregiver. My breathing stopped. I felt my stomach knot up. Was there any escape from this woman? Would my life always be tied to hers? 24 hour care? I couldn't breathe.

BOARDING STABLE RANTS

why barn owners are crazy!

FORWARD

This book was written after 45 years in the business of boarding horses. It was born out of hard work, joys and tears, fights and victories, rescues, puzzelments and bitch sessions.

I hope it will make you smile or laugh. If it makes you angry, maybe I've hit a nerve or fleshed out a truth.

The truth is that it's difficult to be a boarder who has to trust someone else to care for their most precious animal and it's difficult to be a boarding stable owner who has to balance all the aspects of running a business with being an unpaid psychologist.

And now that I've managed to ruffle the feathers of both boarders and boarding stable owners, let's see if I can do some more damage in the following pages...

DEDICATION

This book is dedicated to the memory of my husband, Joel, who firmly believed that horses were livestock until the day we divorced.

NOTE

In this book, I refer to the boarding stable owner and the boarder as "you". I might not be referring directly to you as the subject of my rant but, I could be if the shoe fits!

I'm gonna step on a few toes. I've been in this business too long to be nice about the issues in this book. I've wrangled with them almost every day of my life for the last 45 years and it's time to vent, so put on your shit-kickin' boots and join me!

ROADAPPLES...

TABLE OF CONTENTS

Learn to Ride!
Introducing horse care and riding

TO THE NEW HORSEMAN:

Learn to Ride! is a guide, written for young horsemen, but it has been proven to be useful and fun for new horsemen of any age. I suggest that any new horseman of any age find an instructor to act as a mentor when using this guide.

Please write in this book:
There is a place for your name and places to make notes. There are questions throughout the book about each chapter. You can answer the questions - either with your instructor or at home by yourself. Some questions are about things not discussed in this book. I asked them to make you THINK and to discuss them with your instructor or find the answers online. It's fun to not know something and learn the answer!

With the help of this book, searching online or asking your instructor, you will learn to halter, groom, show a horse in-hand, help tack up your horse and ride a beginner dressage test.

Welcome to the wonderful world of horses!

Charlotte Godfrey

FABULOUS FORWARDS
14 years of forwarding fun!

INTRODUCTION

It was the year 2000 and I didn't know how to turn on a computer. That was fine with my husband. He wanted me at home, taking care of him and pretty much ignorant of the outside world, except for TV news, which was unavoidable since he watched it every night. But I was curious and I requested a computer for Christmas. My husband brought home an old desktop from his workplace with Windows 94 on it. No internet.

I asked my girlfriend, Sandi, to give me a lesson on computers, "Teach me how a computer works," I said. She giggled and rubbed her hands together. "Okay! Welcome to the modern world! This is how you turn it on. Now what do you want to do?"

"I don't know." I said, "Just teach me a little about them." So, she proceeded to tell me that computers are based on files and folders, and my eyes glazed over. First typing, then files and folders? Ugh. I hated typing in high school and barely passed the class. Files and folders? It sounded boring.

But she continued to teach me. Computers, she said, can be highly organized tools. I really like organization. So I learned about files and folders and I became a fairly good typist.

By January, I was longing to be on the internet and find out what the big deal was, so I called a dial-up company and got online. Then the emails started coming in from all my computer savy friends! What a hoot! The fun was unbelievable! So I copied the best forwards, pasted them into files and put them in folders... for fourteen years!

Now it appears that texting is replacing emailing friends and the once enjoyable experience of email has become a slush pile of advertisement and con artist scams. I came to realize that I had enjoyed an "era" which has pretty much passed.

This book is an effort to preserve, in my own way, the fun that emailing once gave us. I urge you to copy some of these forwards and send them to your friends. Have fun!

70+ jokes about aging, sure to make you laugh out loud:

AGING FORWARDS
14 years of forwarding fun!

LIFE BEGINS AT FIFTY

Maybe it's true that life begins at fifty...
But thats when everything else starts to wear out,
fall out, or spread out.

LIFE WITH DUTCH

life with a 20 year old grouchy Amazon parrot

I'm a 76 year old woman who adopted a 20 year old Amazon parrot. I am approaching the end of my life but a 20 year old Amazon parrot is just beginning middle age. I guess I thought I'd have to decide who gets to care for the bird when I'm gone. But, as it turned out, the bird decided that one.

I am retired and living alone in an apartment and I got the bright idea of adopting a parrot. I guess you could say I was lonely and looking for trouble. I found it.

Dutch had been in the same home with his owner, a man, for 20 years. The first owner died and the surviving relatives sent Dutch to a rescue. That should have told me something.

And the name "Dutch" should have also told me something. It's an old fashioned slang word meaning "trouble."

I went to the rescue looking for an African Grey parrot. I owned a Grey and a Amazon when I was younger. Much younger. The Grey was intelligent, talkative and had a gentle nature. The Amazon was aggressive and loud. Maybe I didn't remember that.

Anyway, the rescue didn't have a Grey, but it had an Amazon for adoption: Dutch. I visited with Dutch for a month before adopting him, and he bit me, but only once. It didn't draw blood, and I shrugged it off. The old saying is "If you own a parrot, it's not a question of if you're gonna be bitten, but when."

The surviving relatives, who dropped Dutch off at the rescue, didn't leave a written history. The rescue told me he had been the property of a man for 20 years, preferred men, and was adopted by another man and returned to the rescue after 5 days. That should have told me something. But...

The rescue said the man who adopted him had 3 dogs and Dutch had become aggravated because of them and was returned. That made sense to me at the time, but I realized later that Dutch could make short work of three dogs.

In addition, there was no vet history for Dutch, no evidence that he knew how to speak and his wings were fully clipped.

I don't have any dogs or cats. I live in a small apartment by myself so, I adopted Dutch.It wasn't long before I thought I would have been happier with a pit bull or a tarantula.

THE HORSE CONNECTION part 1

horses, love and loss

I went to work the next day after school, as usual. I grabbed my wheelbarrow and pitchfork and started on the first stall. I was working on the second one when the idiots appeared in the doorway of the stall. I was trapped.

"Hey, thanks for getting the hay for us yesterday," Ray said. "And it was really nice of you to give us the rest of the afternoon off."

I just looked at him while the anger was building up inside me.

"Yeah, Max was a little upset with you, though," Ray said with a smirk on his face. "He thought you were getting a little uppity, taking over like that, and acting like you was the boss. And you owe us," he added, "or else we will tell Max you dumped us just to be a bitch when we left the truck to go pee."

Then Ray turned to Joe. "Wanna go first?"

Joe smiled and shook his head. "Go ahead, bro. You go first."

Ray stepped into the stall. Then he spread his legs and unbuckled his belt.

I didn't ask him what he was doing. I just hit him hard on his stupid head with the business end of my pitchfork. I was really glad it was the old-fashioned metal kind. But Ray wasn't. He crumbled like an empty burlap sack.

Joe was a little slow to react. He just stood there with his mouth open, watching Ray fall. That gave me enough time to grab the wheelbarrow and slam it into his knees. He fell as gracelessly as his bro. Just for fun, I emptied the contents of the wheelbarrow on his face.

I didn't stick around after that. I grabbed my bicycle and went home. It was Friday, so I told my mother we ran out of work early and quit for the day.

I didn't work at the Silver Spur on the weekends. The boys were going to get a couple of days to think about things. I just hoped they were smart enough to figure out that I won't be messed with when I went back to work on Monday.

But Max called my mother and said I was fired.

By then, I guess she had enough of me getting fired, because that's when she decided to get rid of me.

THE HORSE CONNECTION part 3

growing pains

I waited as the guard unlocked the gates. She pushed them open for me, and I walked through to freedom.

"Thanks," I said.

"Don't come back," she joked.

"Not a chance."

I had my suitcase, some money and my life back. Five years gone. A 27-year-old was. My dreams hadn't died, and neither had my anger. But now, thanks to anger management classes, I had the skill to hide it, control it be patient and plan my revenge.

No one met me at the gate. I was alone. My husband divorced me as soon as I was incarcerated. I had only one visitor while I was waiting in the county jail for my trial. Marsha came once and brought me some money. She never came back, but she sent me a few dollars each month through the prison's system of handling an inmate's cash. And I hadn't heard from anyone at Centerline or from the club during the past five years. It was their loss. I wouldn't forget it, either.

The one thing I really missed was horses. I spent my entire life with horses since I was eight years old. I missed my horse Marlboro the most, and I intended to see him soon. That is, I hoped to see him. I hoped Bonnie had kept him at the farm for me, and I hoped she had taken care of his tendon injury, too. At any rate, I intended to find out as soon as possible.

Marlboro was five years older now and should have healed. I hoped he was still being ridden. He was training at Grand Prix when he was injured during turnout in a pasture. Alone. No one seemed to know how he got hurt. That was suspicious, and I still thought it might have been caused by one of the many barn helpers I fired when I worked at Centerline. Barn help? More like barn harm, I thought. Anyway, he should have healed by now.

I shifted my suitcase to my left hand and took a deep breath of free air. It smelled good. But not fresh. I could detect diesel fumes and asphalt in it, but it smelled good, anyway. Prison air smelled like sweat and urine. When we got outside for 2 hours a day, the air smelled like sweat and cigarette smoke. I didn't smoke and I used deodorant. Yes, diesel and asphalt definitely smelled better.

No one was meeting me, and I didn't have a ride. I walked away from the Women's Huron Valley Correctional Facility and onto Bemis Road. I headed east on Bemis because I knew it would cross 23 and then connect with I-94. After I got on 23, I walked backwards and stuck out my thumb when I saw a tractor trailer approaching. I was still skinny and attractive. I got a ride.

The trucker who picked me up was middle-aged, had a day-old beard and smelled sweaty. "Where are you headed?" he asked when I got in.

"Port Huron."

"Well, you're in luck. I'm headed to Canada through Port Huron." The trucker put his turn signal on and eased back into traffic.

"Great." I looked in the back of his cab. It had a bedroll in it. "You sleep back there?"

"Sometimes. Sometimes I use it for other things," he grinned, but got no response from me, so he said,"Why are you hitching? What's your story?"

"I just got out of prison."

The trucker's eyebrows shot up. I could see that I had earned a little respect. "What were you in for?"

"Murder. I killed a woman."

The trucker looked at me. "How? Did you shoot her?"

"No, I beat her to death."

"Wow," he laughed nervously. "You must have been really mad."

"I still am."

About the Author:

Charlotte Godfrey's first horse was her Grandpop's mule, Maggie, who she jumped bareback - until Pop found her on the ground after jumping an obstacle under Granny's wire clothes line. When he discovered that she wasn't decapitated, he forbade her to jump and bought her a horse who tried to kill her in other ways. That horse, who knew several ways of getting rid of children, taught her about self-preservation and confirmed in her a life-long love of horses and dressage.

photograph by Michael Sexton

Her next horse, after a child, college, marriage, divorce and re-marriage (in that order, but repeat a few steps...) was a Quarter Horse named Oliver, who was obtained by blackmailing her husband and threatening the owner. After Charlotte added 2 more horses to the board bill, her husband decided that it would be cheaper and more tax-advantageous to buy property and build their own boarding stable! He built a barn, purchased a horse trailer, dug a pond, constructed an outdoor arena, an indoor arena, more stalls...and so on...

Running a boarding stable proved to be such a delightful way to lose money that, after her divorce, Charlotte and 2 unfortunate partners: Mike and her mother, Milly, joined up to buy an even bigger boarding stable.

Charlotte is pictured above with her horse, Gotsno, or "Mr. Wonderful," as he prefers to be known...

If you enjoyed this book, please leave a review.

www.ingramcontent.com/pod-product-compliance
Lightning Source LLC
Chambersburg PA
CBHW051412170626
46809CB00006B/2136